CARING FOR LOVED ONES AT HOME

CARING FOR LOVED ONES AT HOME

Harry van Bommel

Illustrations by Diane Huson

Published by
ROBERT POPE FOUNDATION

Distributed by
LANCELOT PRESS LIMITED

Illustrations by Diane Huson

COVER ILLUSTRATION:
An original work of art (actual size) by Tom Forrestall

ISBN 0-88999-606-7
Published 1996

Distributed by
LANCELOT PRESS LTD.
P.O. Box 425, Hantsport, Nova Scotia B0P 1P0
Telephone 902 684-9129   Fax 902 684-3685

ACKNOWLEDGEMENTS

I am grateful to the following people for their editorial advice: **Cathryn Allen**, Program Manager of the Palliative Care Program, Camp Hill Medical Centre, Halifax, Nova Scotia; **Gloria Repetto** and **Florence Bell**, Head Nurse and Nursing Supervisor, respectively at Victoria General Hospital, Halifax; **Members of the Canadian Home Care Association**; **Dr. Ina Cummings**, Medical Director for Palliative Care at Camp Hill Medical Centre; **Shari Douglas**, Home Care Case Manager in Owen Sound, Ontario; **Diane Huson**, illustrator, Whitby, Ontario; **Connie Smith**, Long-Term Care Coordinator for Kincardine and District General Hospital, Ontario; **Deb Thivierge**, Human Services Consultant and partner in Paradigm Partners, Toronto, Ontario; **Glenna Thornhill**, Home Care Nurse, Camp Hill Medical Centre; **Dorothy Woodward**, retired home support worker, Parksville, British Columbia. My sincerest thanks and love to **Janet Klees** who helped provide home care to my father and who edits all of my work.

I am grateful to **William Pope** for requesting and encouraging the production of this book. Our joint aim is to provide information that will help families, like ours, deal even more effectively with the care they provide their loved ones.

I would like to thank NC Press Limited for their support in allowing portions of my book *Choices for People Who Have a Terminal Illness, Their Families and Their Caregivers* (1993) to be reproduced here.

To contact the author for speaking engagements, contact:

PSD Consultants
11 Miniot Circle
Scarborough, Ontario M1K 2K1
CANADA
(416) 264-4665

In memory of Moeder, Vader and Opa, with love and gratitude; and dedicated to Janet, Bram and Joanna who share this continuing adventure.

CONTENTS

INTRODUCTION

This book is meant to help people who need extra health care support at home. It does not matter if the person is recovering from an illness or surgery or whether they have a more chronic or palliative condition. The tips in this book will help both that person and the family members and friends who are providing support.

The simple line drawings are meant to illustrate specific points in the instructions. Use them as guides to help you practice each of the different techniques. Remember, you are not trying to be the perfect professional nurse. Rather you are trying to be helpful to someone you care about and these techniques will help you do exactly that. Be proud of your accomplishments. You are making a real difference in someone's life. Without you, they might not be able to stay in the comfort of their own home. When you are trying a new technique, don't be shy to ask the person you are helping to tell you what is working and what you might try to do differently. You are not doing this alone. You are working together with the person you are caring for so that both of you feel satisfied with the results.

The book is not a description of Home Care Programs across North America. Wherever you live, there is probably some form of Home Care Program available through your health care system. Find out at the hospital, through your family doctor, or through your telephone directory about services that are available in your area. A Home Care Case Manager can be an invaluable resource to help you get the support you need to stay at home.

I helped both of my parents and grandfather to live at home until they died. I have also helped other loved ones who were ill, recovering from an illness or getting their strength back after giving birth. During those times I was reminded of the few practical skills I really had and how much better I could help others if I only knew more. A book like this would have been very helpful. I hope you find it helpful as well. I also hope the information will help you to know what kinds of questions to ask to get the kinds of support you or a loved one need.

The cover painting of this book is of two hands — one of an elder and one of a younger person. Either one of these people could be giving or receiving care at home. We must always remember that everyone in our lives has gifts to offer when they support each other. It does not matter whether they are young or old, woman or man, family member or friend or if they are disabled in some way. It is in recognizing their gifts, encouraging their efforts, asking them for help when we need it, and sharing in their compassion that we all participate in the human family.

Sincere Best Wishes

HARRY VAN BOMMEL
Scarborough, Ontario

NOTE: This is a short book. Therefore, we cannot cover every kind of health care situation you, or a loved one, may be experiencing. ***Adapt the information in this book to meet your needs.*** Some people who use this book will need it for only a short time. Others may need it for several months or longer. ***If you cannot find what you need in this book, ask your Home Care Case Manager, family doctor or visiting home nurse for more specific information.*** There is a lot of specific information out there and these people can help you get it quickly. Also look in the recommended resource list at the end of this book and your local library for further information.

What to Do in an Emergency

1. Discuss with your physician and health care team who should be called for what type of emergency. Keep a list of their names and telephone numbers by the telephone. What may originally feel like an emergency may only require some telephone help from your physician, nurse, social worker or home care case manager.

2. In almost all other emergency situations where you are unable to deal with whatever is happening, you should CALL 911 or your local hospital, fire department, or ambulance service.

3. DO NOT CALL 911 if someone has died a natural, expected death at home. Call your family physician, instead, who can tell you what you should do.

If you are expecting to care for someone at home, and have enough time to plan for that situation (e.g. someone is having surgery in six months, a baby will be born in the next nine months) then take an emergency first aid course or upgrading program. There are also family health care programs offered through local organizations including St. John Ambulance, The Red Cross, Community Colleges and others. The more you know what to do in an emergency situation, the more comfortable you will feel and the more control you will have during the situation.

As with all good planning, you should think about what you will do in different situations BEFORE they happen. Just as we should plan our escape route from our home if there is a fire, we should also know what to do if someone gets seriously ill at home. The more we think about these situations in advance, the more we will act naturally and be relatively calm if the situation ever happens.

Home Care Examples

The following are some stories of how different people met their home care needs. For Jennifer, all of her home care was provided by family, friends and familiar health care providers. Francis needed a mix of family and special home care programs offered through the health care system. Jorge has to rely, almost exclusively, on the professional services offered through Home Care Programs and other community organizations.

Home Birth

Jennifer has decided to have a home birth if her pregnancy continues to go well. Her husband, Joe, is a little nervous but agrees as long as the midwives teach him what to do if there is an emergency in the middle of the night. As Jennifer's pregnancy continues, there are some typical ups and downs and concerns. All of these are met with compassion and honest communication between Jennifer, Joe, their midwives and their family physician.

When the baby announces it is time to arrive, Jennifer and Joe call their midwives and their two friends, Susan and Margaret, and prepare their bedroom for the birth. Jennifer has time for a hot shower while Joe gets their young son (Daniel) ready for a day with his "Auntie" Margaret. When Margaret arrives, she takes Daniel out for a morning full of preplanned activity. When Susan arrives, she begins to make some muffins for everyone and prepares tea and other "comfort foods" for Jennifer, Joe and the midwives. When the midwives arrive, they have all the equipment one would find in a community hospital for deliveries, and they equip the room using towels to cover equipment that will likely not be needed. They come in and out of the room to check on Jennifer, but for the most part, leave Jennifer and Joe together.

When the baby is ready to come out, Joe helps support Jennifer while the midwives talk Jennifer through the process.

It takes different body positions, careful attention to breathing and Jennifer's loving attention to her baby. With the midwives gentle assistance the baby is born at 12:12 p.m. just in time for Daniel to see his new baby sister. The midwives help clean up the room (leave it cleaner than when they arrived) and one stays during the afternoon to make sure that everything is going well. Joe, other family members, friends and the midwives continue to provide home care supports to Jennifer and the new baby for the next few days and weeks until everyone is strong again. Joe helped Jennifer wash herself in bed (she had to stay for three days). He also helped her begin to move around the house and go to the washroom. Jennifer, Joe and Daniel are all proud of Maria's arrival in the safety and comfort of their own home.

Recovering at Home

Francis lives on a farm about 25 miles from the nearest hospital. One night she wakes up in extreme pain. Her husband, Willy, rushes her to hospital where she undergoes emergency surgery. After about a week in the hospital, Francis is able to go home to recover. Willy has to spend most of the time out in the fields as this is harvest time. However, he always gets back to prepare Francis a good lunch and supper before going out to work a little longer.

Their daughter, Marion, still lives at home and is able to help around the house when she is not at work. Marion makes sure that Francis takes the right medication at the right times, helps her mother do some simple washing up in bed, and helps her to the washroom. She cleans the linen on the bed regularly so that Francis is comfortable. Marion tries to be home when the nurse arrives so she and her mother can ask the nurse specific questions and record the nurse's answers. She cooks and freezes some meals so that her father only has to warm them up the next day.

Every day during that first week at home, a visiting nurse came to change Francis' dressing. The surgery was major, so

Francis was unable to take a bath, so the visiting nurse gave her a sponge bath in bed. After the first week, the nurse only comes every third day for another two weeks. By then Francis is able to take care of all her own personal care and will be back to full strength in another three weeks of taking it easy.

Long-Term Care at Home

Jorge is 82 years old and lives in a Home for the Aged in a big city. His wife died 11 years ago and he has no family living nearby. He has difficulty getting around so he uses a motorized scooter. His Home Care Case Manager arranged for him to get his bed raised so that it is easier to get in and out of it alone at night. She also arranged to have Jorge's bathtub adapted with strong holding bars to make it easier to use. An adaptive toilet seat is also used so that Jorge does not have to bend as far to sit down.

A nurse comes every three days to help him get a good shower and wash his full head of grey hair. A homemaker comes once a week to give his single-room apartment a good cleaning and do some of his laundry. The homemaker also prepares a nutritious lunch and supper for him. Some of Jorge's other meals come through the community group Meals on Wheels and the rest he cooks himself or eats with friends in his building.

A volunteer comes to visit Jorge for a few hours every week. Jorge and David chat about common interests, play some cribbage and make plans for special occasions like the winter holidays, shopping trips, drives in the country or a simple stroll around the building. David understands some basic home care skills, so he is able to help Jorge go to the washroom, help review the charts left by the visiting nurses, or give him a wonderful massage just before leaving for the night. They have become friends over the past few years and David invites Jorge to his home once every month or two to share in some family activities.

Jorge had to go to hospital suddenly because of a heart problem. Before he returned home, an occupational therapist visited his apartment to see if there was other equipment that could be brought in to help Jorge with his daily tasks. Home Care arranged to bring in a few more metal bars that Jorge could hold onto in his kitchenette and by his bed. They also recommended that Jorge subscribe to an emergency telephone signal that he would wear around his neck. If he fell or couldn't get to a phone, he would just press this button and a signal would go into a business that would call a neighbour to check on him.

Jorge is able to stay in his home because of the services available in his community. If he becomes less able to care for himself, however, he will require further services not available to him in his own home. Since he has no family or friends near by able to help him, he will need to go into a long-term care facility or nursing home. This frightens Jorge but he continues to hope that it will never come to that for him, as it has for so many of his friends who used to live in the same building.

• • • • • •

These stories illustrate just some of the situations that might arise where someone requires extra supports at home. Other situations may include parents caring for a child with disabilities, adult children caring for an ailing parent at home, a partner caring for a loved one with cancer or AIDS, or a family caring for someone who wants to live at home until they die.

Whatever the circumstances, providing care for a loved one at home involves some of the basic skills described in this book. If possible, it helps to do some of the caregiving for someone in hospital where nurses and other professionals can teach you specific techniques. It makes caring for someone at home a lot easier if you have had the chance to practice under the supervision of skilled caregivers.

Understanding How Illness Affects Someone Who is Ill, and Their Family

Whenever I ask people if they would like to be a patient — they all answer no! No one likes to be sick. Few of us enjoy having others take care of us except to be spoiled for a few days when we have a flu.

Longer-term care can be quite frustrating for people and for those who care for them. Most of us would prefer to give the care than to receive it. We have been brought up in the last 50 years to believe that allowing people to care for you is a burden on them. For those of us who have cared for others for quite some time, we recognize that often it is an honor and a pleasure to care for someone we love. There are times of great love, intimacy and laughter. There are also times of frustration and exhaustion. Often the difficulties do not come from taking care of someone else but because we forget to take care of ourselves or we do not ask for enough support from family, friends and community services.

The people who spend most of their time caring for someone they love need physical, emotional, spiritual and informational supports just like the person who is getting home care. We often do not know how to ask for these supports and many people do not know how to offer them — so the needed support is not there. One of the last sections of this book, *Creating Your Own Support Team*, is one way to change that. Modify the list of suggestions to meet your own needs. *People generally love to help if they know it is only for a few hours every week or two. They will cut lawns, get groceries, walk your dog, pick people up at the airport, or prepare a frozen meal you can use whenever you want.* You only have to give people an excuse to help and most are more than happy to do it. They want a specific task or duty to perform to show they care and respect the person who is getting home care.

There are a few other things you can do to make home care more successful:

1. Understand that your lives have changed for a while and that you will not be able to do everything you used to, or when you used to do it. Recognize as well (and this is just as important) that you will be doing new things that will enrich your lives, make a real difference in the lives of your loved ones and will help you remember what is truly important in life. This is a time of both giving and receiving. This is also a time that will make you stronger if you get the supports and information you need.

2. Understand that both the person who is receiving care at home and those giving the care must work to help each other. In other words, if your mother is at home sick and the rest of the family is helping, you must all share in supporting each other. Your mother must recognize that she is still your mother and has gifts to offer you even though she is sick. She still needs to be treated as a mother rather than a sick person. She still needs to offer her motherly advice and wisdom. She can still participate in her own care, to her best ability, while also doing things to provide support to her family. As much as she can, she should continue to offer her gifts of favorite recipes, her needlework or writing letters, or her enjoyment of singing or playing an instrument. She has not changed in basic personality, and how she dealt with problems in the past is probably how she will deal with her illness. The same holds true for all who care for her.

   She must not expect service that one gets from servants just as you cannot expect to provide that kind of service most of the time. While she is being the most helpful person she can be, you need to recognize that you would not want to change places with her and that she is going through some difficult times. Working together and communicating honestly will provide each of you the support you need. If you do not have that kind of relationship, you may need some help to improve the relationship you have. No one is a servant and no one is the master. You are all in this situation together doing the best you can with the knowledge and skills you have right now.

3. You will need to plan ahead to meet the changes in your lives. If you feel overwhelmed with everything that is happening, ask for help from your home care coordinator, family doctor, or friends. Ask them to help you schedule your activities differently so that there is time to rest, relax and think rather than rush, rush all the time. Other people have done this too and we can all learn from their experiences. Perhaps there are self-help support groups in your area to provide extra information and encouragement.

4. Both the person who is ill and the family members may need more knowledge and skills to give the necessary supports to each other. Learn as much as you can from this book and others listed in the Reference List. The best people to learn from are the visiting home nurses so stay in the room with them as they nurse your loved one. Ask questions and offer to help so that you can practice the skills you will need.

5. Try to keep as many of your typical contacts as you can. Neither the person nor the family members should isolate themselves completely from those who love them. Your other family, friends and neighbors can provide you with the kind of emotional and spiritual supports we all need. Again, they may not know how to offer, so ask them over for a tea or take some time away from home to meet them somewhere else for a little break. If you do not know anyone who will stay with your loved one at home while you go out, ask your home care coordinator, visiting home nurse or family doctor for some volunteer services in

your community that may be able to help. There are also some organizations that provide what is called "respite care" to family members to give them some free time. Ideally the person who is ill should not have to leave home to give their family members a rest. It is better if the family is given an opportunity to have a weekend away or some similar time off.

6. Understand that people's personalities do not change very much. If someone was very happy and family-oriented before their illness, they will probably remain that way now. If someone was quite unhappy and grouchy before the illness, they will not suddenly become happy and enjoy everyone's company. This is just as true for family members caring for someone. The more we understand this basic truth, the less we will be frustrated when people do not suddenly change to suit our needs. When there are significant changes in personality one should check about possible side effects from the medication or a physical cause (e.g. dementias, brain cancer).

7. Each of us deals with stress differently. This is just as true with the stress of an illness or some of the stress of caring for someone else. The more you recognize how someone has dealt with stress in the past the more you can help them deal positively with this stress. Whatever people have done in the past, they will probably do again. Listening to them and helping them to sort out other possible ways of dealing with the stress will help you both.

8. Few people enjoy hearing about how someone else has had the "exact same illness or condition and you should have seen how bad they had it!" These kinds of comparisons are not very helpful. Avoid comparing people's individual condition or illness and how well they are dealing with it to other people's experiences.

9. When you have time away from caregiving or receiving care, you may want to join others to find ways to support those in the community who have longer-term care commitments. You may also begin to discuss with community leaders, employers and politicians how we can adapt our systems to provide the economic stability and personal supports that people need who are caring for others, full-time, in their home. This group of mostly women is saving our country billions of dollars in institutional care but we often isolate them, force them to quit jobs they enjoy and provide them with little physical, emotional, spiritual and information support to care for loved ones at home. You only have to imagine what it is like to care for someone with dementia at home, or someone with physical disabilities requiring round-the-clock care, to understand how important it is that we all support each other in caring for loved ones at home.

From personal experiences I know that home care has many positive moments and some frustrating and angry ones. This is typical. You have all had jobs, relationships and vacations that had positive and negative experiences as part of them. That is reality for most of us. Home care is no different. The greatest predictor of how much you get out of this experience is whether or not you believe that home care is a wonderful opportunity for the person and family alike to share in a common, life-defining experience. If you believe that and if you take the time and effort (both the person who is ill or recovering and the rest of the family) to make sure that many of the physical, emotional, spiritual and informational needs are met; then you will be fine. When you experience difficulties, talk to your home care coordinator, visiting home nurse, family doctor and other family members and friends to get their help.

Adapting Your Home and Getting the Right Equipment

When someone at home needs some extra health care it may be helpful to change your home in some of the following ways.

Perhaps the person will need to stay in bed or is unable to move around very much. They can either do that in their own bedroom or they may prefer the bed be moved to a more common room, like a living room or den. In this way they can stay part of the daily activities of the family. It may be helpful to have the bed near to a bathroom so the person does not have far to travel. Carpeted floors (not throw rugs) help make sure the person is less likely to slip and fall and also cuts down on noise. Being near a window and sunlight is very enjoyable for many people as well as being surrounded by favorite pictures, music and pets. The room should be comfortably warm or cool depending on the season, with good air ventilation (without causing drafts).

Some furniture that is helpful to have in arm's reach of a comfortable bed includes:

✓ **a small table** (same height as bed) where the person can put their medicine, snacks, radio, writing paper, etc. Even better is a table with a few drawers (like in a hospital) where a person can put some personal items like comb, brush, toothbrush, mirror, box of tissues, urinal or bed pan.

✓ a comfortable **armchair** nearby where they can sit, perhaps look out a window, watch television or read. The chair should be high enough to get in to and out of fairly easily.

✓ a sturdy **footstool** to help the person get in and out of bed if the bed is high.

✓ a small **bell, intercom or buzzer** to call for help.

✓ something fresh to drink, especially **water** and some favorite **snacks**.

✓ a place to put magazines, books, television converter, knitting or other leisure things.

✓ **good lighting** for talking with people, reading, watching television.

✓ a sturdy **food tray** to help make eating more comfortable in bed.

✓ a **telephone**.

You may also need some special equipment to help you. Talk with your Home Care Case Manager to arrange for the things that you need to borrow, rent or buy. These may include:

❑ an adjustable bed (similar to a hospital bed),

❑ a bed table high enough to fit over one's knees lying in bed,

- ☐ a bed cradle to protect a sensitive part of the body from the weight or movement of sheets and blankets,
- ☐ a back rest to help a person sit up in bed,
- ☐ sheepskin padding or pillows, foam or sponge pads to help a person prevent bed sores,
- ☐ incontinence pads for under the person in bed in case there is any urine or feces incontinence,
- ☐ a foot board made of strong cardboard, or hard pillow or something else quite creative to allow the person in bed to push against it so that they can keep their body position comfortable. Often people who are sitting up in bed end up sliding down the bed to uncomfortable positions.

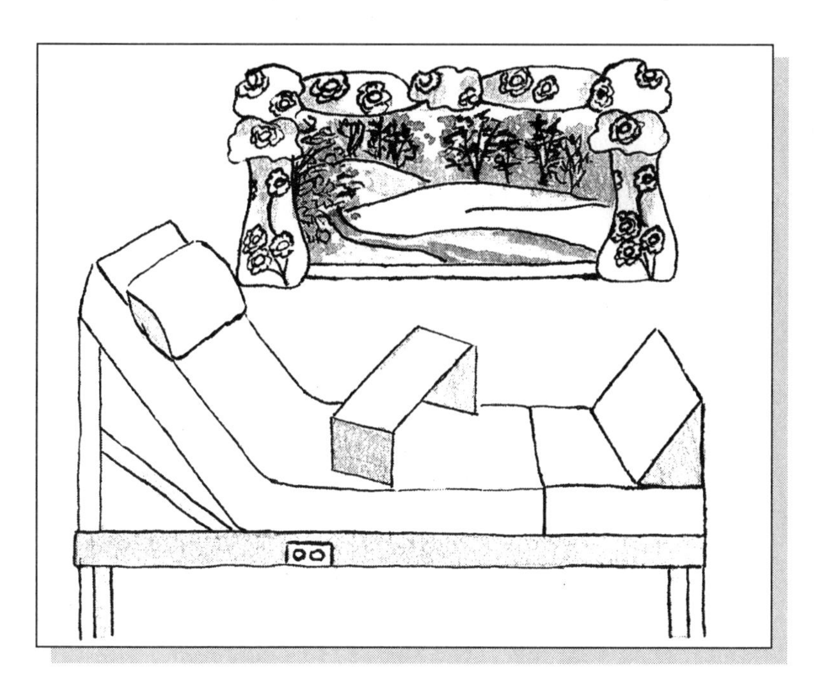

Helping People to Get Around

A good deal of your time may be spent helping the person get in or out of bed, walking around their home or helping them get to their bathroom. You have seen relatively short nurses help people around the hospital so you know that you do not need to be very tall or physically strong. You do need to be smart about what you do so that you do not hurt yourself. Ask your visiting home nurse for tips — they are the experts. Here are some specific tips that might help as well:

✓ Keep your feet and toes pointed straight ahead with your weight evenly divided on both feet.

Proper Lifting Technique

- ✓ You need to stand as straight as you can, keep your head up, shoulders down and knees slightly bent.
- ✓ When lifting someone, you should have your head, shoulders and hips form a straight line. You need to bend your knees and keep your back as straight as possible when lifting. Have your feet about 30 cm (one foot) apart for best stability.
- ✓ Learn a few stretching exercises for your legs, arms, back and stomach muscles and practice them before you do any lifting or assisting.
- ✓ The closer you are to the person or object you are lifting, the less strain on your muscles.
- ✓ Make sure the area you will be lifting or walking in does not have anything in the way (e.g. children's toys, throw rugs) and that it is not slippery.
- ✓ Wear comfortable, low-heel shoes and loose-fitting clothes.

Moving Someone in Bed

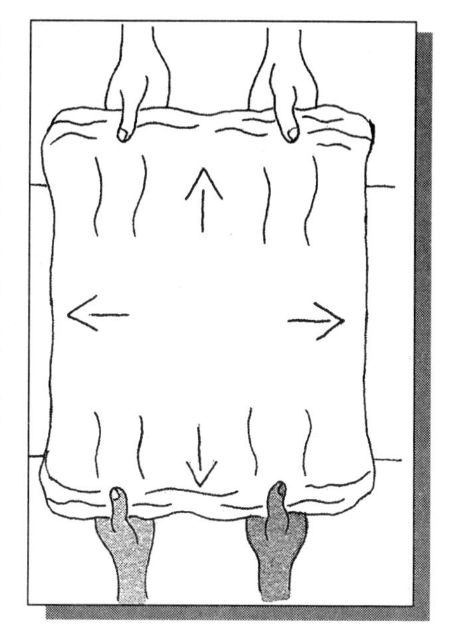

The greatest invention in the world (or so it seemed to me at the time I was taking care of my parents) is a draw sheet. This is just a regular sheet folded several times and placed sideways on the bed. The person lays on top with the sheet under their shoulders and hips. With a person on either side of the bed, each grabs the sheet at the same time and together they can lift the person up to move them closer to the head or the foot of the bed. This is very helpful when someone is sitting up in bed and they keep sliding to the foot of the bed. If they cannot move themselves, the draw sheet is perfect to move them without a lot of pulling or pushing on their skin. You can also use the draw sheet to help turn someone onto their side by placing one end of the draw sheet over the person and pulling it towards you.

Helping Turn Someone in Bed

Other than the draw sheet, you can also help a person turn in bed in the following way:

1. Have their far arm across their chest towards you.
2. Bend their far leg at the knee while their foot still rests on the mattress. Bring the bent leg towards you. As you do this, their far shoulder will naturally start to move towards you through the leverage of the leg. Reach over with your hand to guide their shoulder towards you comfortably and safely. This will put the person on their side with their bent knee giving extra security.
3. Place pillows to support their back and, if necessary, between their legs for added comfort. Adjust the head pillow as needed.

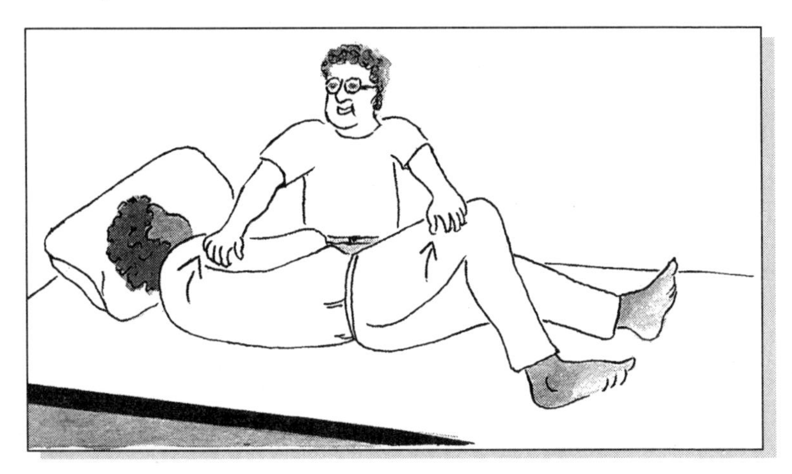

Getting Someone Out of Bed and into a Chair

1. Put a safe and solid chair with armrests next to the bed facing you. The chair should be high enough to make it easy for the person to get into it and out again.
2. Raise the head of the bed as high as it will go. Help move the person's legs over the side of the bed. Give them a moment to rest as they may be a bit dizzy at first sitting up after lying down so long.
3. Help the person put on their slippers or shoes (or do it when they are still lying down if they cannot help).
4. If the bed is too high, put a strong foot rest by the bed to help the person step down comfortably.
5. Help the person slide forward to the edge of the bed so their feet are touching the floor or foot stool.
6. Face the person with your foot that is nearest the chair one step behind the other. This will allow you to turn easily in the direction of the chair.

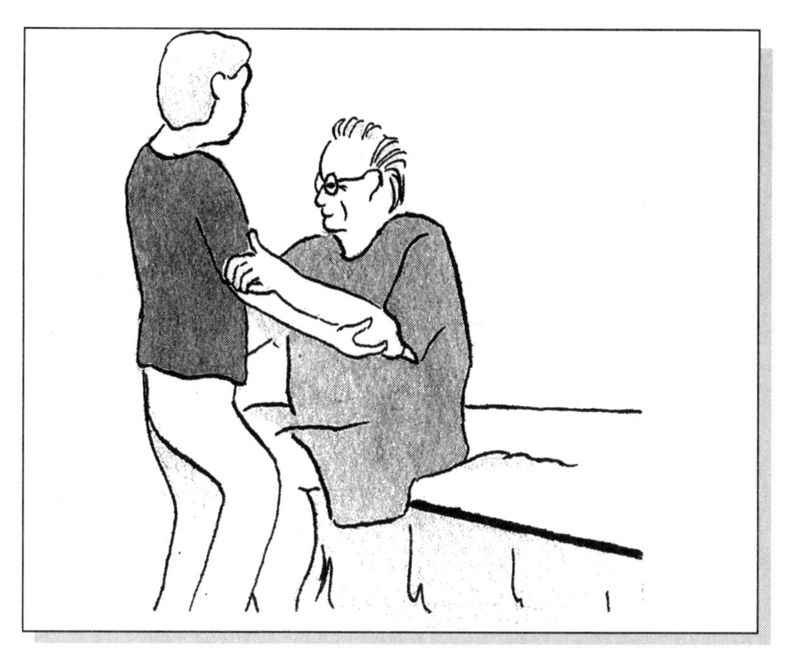

7. Have the person brace themselves with their hands around your elbows while your hands hold them under their elbows for leverage.

8. Help the person slide off the bed.

9. Bend your knees and press your forward knee against the outside of the person's opposite knee. Let them catch their breath and balance themselves as they stand.

10. Let the person shuffle backward towards the chair if they can and help them lower themselves. If they need help, pivot them using the pressure on their knee, and then lower them into the chair.

From a Chair into Bed

Reverse the instructions from above making sure the person helps with as much of the moving as possible. As well, make sure the chair, foot stool and bed won't move while you are helping the person.

Walking

✓ Help the person stand from their bed or a chair. You can offer extra support either by holding them under their arm or elbow.

✓ When you walk together, have your closest arm around their waist and the other hand can hold their nearest elbow or hand for extra support. Stay close to the person so that your hip can give them extra stability.

NOTE:

If the person can no longer stand and they begin to slowly slump onto the floor, bend your own knees and help them glide against your body and down your knee to the floor. After they have rested, you can put a chair in front of them and help them kneel in front of it for support as you slowly bring them to a standing position. Let them rest one hand on the

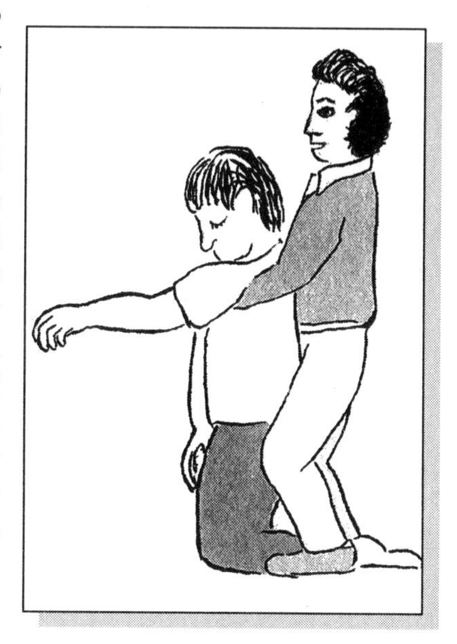

chair with which they will push themselves up. Put your strongest forearm under their bent free forearm. Bend at the knees and try to keep your back in good alignment (although this is difficult in this position). Lift up with your arm at the same time the person pushes up from the chair. Turn them slowly so that they can sit down in the chair for a more comfortable rest. If they cannot get up, wait for help to bring them back to bed or try to slide the chair to the bed. At all times, remember to safeguard your own back since you will not be at all helpful if you injure yourself.

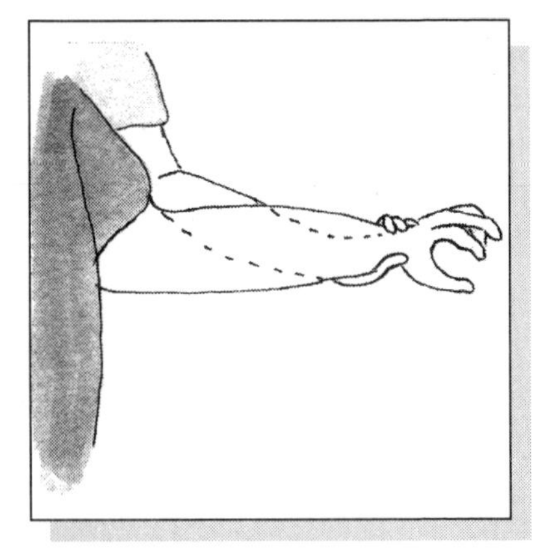

Supported Lying Positions

People need to rest in different lying positions so that they do not put too much pressure on any single body part or skin area. People can sit up, lay down or lay on their sides as they normally do for a sleep. A few quick tips:

Sitting Up

The head should be raised about 45º-60º with small pillows under their head, lower back and under their knees (or raise the foot portion of the bed). This position is helpful for eating, using a bedpan or urinal and helps improve the person's heart and lung work. If the person likes a large pillow, place it lengthwise to support their upper back, shoulders and head. It may help to have a footboard at the bottom of their feet to allow them to push up a little as they will naturally slide down in bed over time.

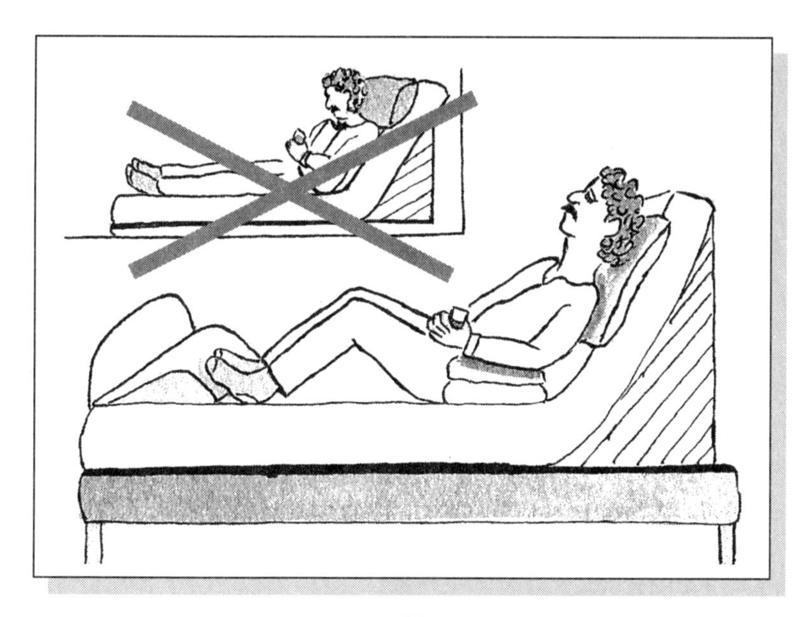

Lying Down

With the person in the center of the bed, put a pillow under their shoulders, neck and head. Another pillow can go under their lower back for extra support and a rolled up towel or smaller pillow under their ankles and knees. The person may also enjoy pillows under the upper arms and hands. Follow the person's wishes and change pillow positions as requested.

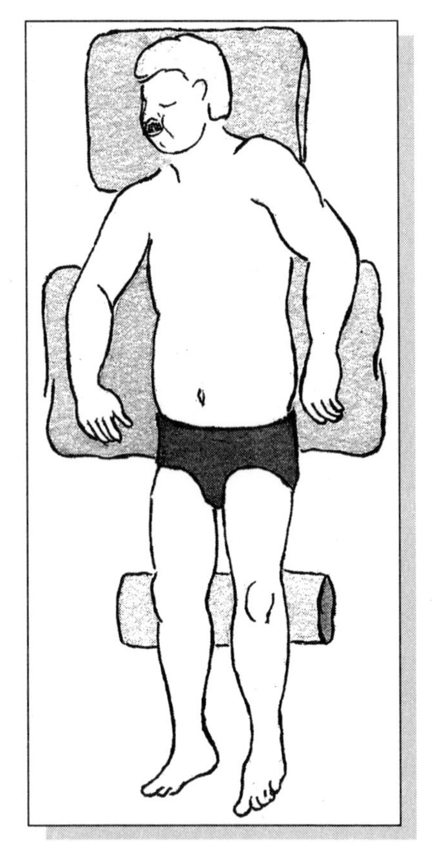

Lying on Side

When you look at a person lying on their side, you should see the same body position as if they were standing with their top leg bent up. The back is in line with the straight leg with pillows under the head, top arm and bent leg. Pillows are also often rolled along their back for extra support.

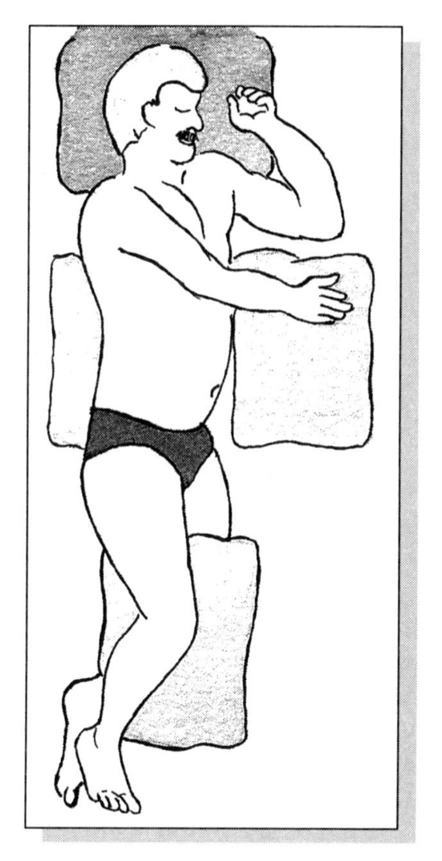

Using a Bedpan or Urinal

None of us enjoy having to use a bedpan or urinal. No matter how hard we try, it is an unnatural feeling and not all that comfortable. However, it is necessary sometimes. After you have helped the person with the equipment, give them some privacy and wait for them to call you for help again. Leave a clean bedpan or urinal and toilet paper close to the bed so that the person, if able, can use it themselves and just call you when they are done.

Specific Tips

Find out if they can use a commode beside the bed. A commode is a portable toilet that looks like a chair. It will allow many people to go to the toilet without them having to travel far. There are various types including ones on wheels and ones with removable arms. Your visiting home nurse, Home Care Case Manager, or family doctor can help you decide which is best.

NOTE: People who are receiving narcotic pain medication may have difficulty with bowel functions (especially with constipation). Any difficulties should be reported to one's family doctor or visiting home nurse immediately to prevent the problem from getting worse. People need to continue using the right dose of pain medication so that they can remain relatively pain free and alert but they also need help controlling any side effects of that medication.

If they cannot use a commode, follow these tips:

✓ Make sure you get the right kind of bedpan or urinal. There are different models for different purposes and you should get the kind that is most comfortable for your specific purpose.

✓ Make sure the bedpan or urinal is clean, warm (you can rinse it with hot water), and dry.
✓ Wash your hands thoroughly and dry them with a clean towel.
✓ You may want to put some talcum powder on the top of the bedpan so it doesn't stick to a person's skin.
✓ Once they are using the bedpan or urinal, you can raise the head of the bed to help them feel more comfortable. Make sure the foot of the bed is down so that urine will run into the urinal and not pour out by mistake.
✓ Make sure the person is wiped clean and dry.
✓ Cover bedpan or urinal before removing to prevent spilling. Empty in the toilet and clean. If you rinse with cold water and baking soda it helps keep the equipment odour free.
✓ Wash your hands and help the person to wash theirs.
✓ Urinating and having bowel movements in such a public way can be major sources of embarrassment and frustration for people. They should not have to wait to use the equipment or to have it taken away when they are done. Anything you can do to help people maintain their sense of control at this time will be an invaluable gift.
✓ People do not have to have a bowel movement everyday to be healthy. It varies from person to person. They will know if the frequency of their bowel movements is normal or abnormal.
✓ Menstruating women should have all the supplies and assistance they need. Again ask them what they need and what kind of help would be appreciated and who they prefer to help them.

Helping Someone onto a Bedpan

✓ If they can help: have them lay on their back, bend their knees so their feet are flat on the mattress and ask them to lift their buttocks while you put the bedpan under them.
✓ If they prefer, they can roll onto the bedpan: have the

person roll onto their side; place the bedpan against their buttocks and ask them to roll onto their back.

✓ If they cannot lift themselves or roll onto a bedpan, assist them to roll onto their side. They may be able to tell you how to help them. Place an incontinence pad on the mattress (if there is not one already) and put the bedpan on the mattress in the correct spot (often a little dent in the mattress where person was laying) and assist them to roll onto the bedpan. You may need to adjust it a little for comfort.

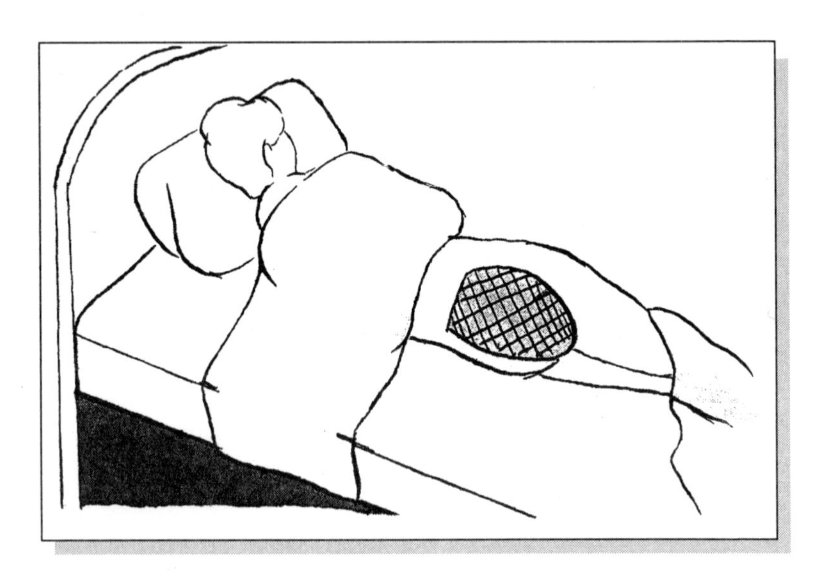

If Someone is Incontinent of Urine or Feces

Incontinence means that the person cannot control their bladder or bowel movements. Odour problems, infections or rashes may develop if the person does not regularly change and keep dry. Their skin care becomes especially important at this point to prevent painful bed sores and other uncomfortable skin conditions.

- ✓ Get specific advice from a dietician, visiting home nurse, Home Care Case Manager or your family doctor.
- ✓ Put a piece of plastic under the bottom sheet of the bed.
- ✓ Use incontinence pads or a clean towel under the person in bed. Change as needed. Reusable incontinence pads or towels should be placed in a sealable container until they are washed. Wash the container with a disinfectant and air out regularly to diminish odour. Sometimes having a vinegar and water solution in the container helps minimize odour as well. Non-reusable incontinence pads should be sealed into an airtight garbage bag and kept outdoors and away from the person's room. Oranges with cloves stuck in them, and left in the room, can also reduce odours.
- ✓ Make sure the person's skin remains clean and dry. Use soapy water and pat as needed. You may also want to use a water-resistant cream to protect the skin. Bed sores are frequently a result of damp skin and poor blood circulation. They are extremely painful and dangerous. Anything you do to keep the skin clean, dry and massaged (to get equal blood flow) will help immeasurably. You will also need to keep bed clothes dry at all times.
- ✓ Pyjama bottoms are not very practical. Long T-shirts, pyjama tops or oversized flannel shirts are quite comfortable. Socks may also help keep someone warm in cool temperatures.
- ✓ The person may want to use adult diapers to keep dry and comfortable and to allow them to get out of bed and walk around for a bit for exercise. Check to see if these, and other supplies, are covered by your local Home Care Program.

Helping with a Bath or Shower

When the person can go into the bath or shower you may find the following tips useful:

✓ Helping people to stand up or sit/lie down can be very difficult on your own body. It is important to remember all the rules of lifting and leaning over that you were taught in school. Remember to bend at the knees when you are picking up an object and keep your back as straight as possible. Remember, as well, that the closer you are to the person or object you are lifting, the less strain you put on your lower back, arms and legs. Some regular squatting exercises will help strengthen your legs and lower back.

✓ If you get quite sore by helping someone get up or down, ask your family doctor, visiting home nurse, occupational therapist, or chiropractor to give you clearer instructions of how to lift someone properly so that you do not continue to hurt yourself.

✓ Help the person into the bath or shower, making sure you bend your knees slightly and keep your back as straight as you can.

✓ If the person is able to help themselves more, you can help them sit on the side of the tub (on a warm, non-slip towel or mat), help them swing their legs over and assist them to ease into the tub. Reverse the procedure when they want to get out.

✓ Make sure the bath or shower has a non-slip bath mat. If the person needs assistance for weeks or months, it may be wise to adapt your bath or shower with handles and other safety aids. Check with an occupational or physiotherapist through your Home Care Program.

✓ If the person prefers a shower, rent or borrow a bath chair or use a water resistant chair so they can sit down comfortably. Your Home Care Program may be able to arrange this.

✓ The person may feel more comfortable if their genital area is covered. You can use a short apron or modified towel with velcro tabs so the person has the privacy they want.

✓ Before the person goes into the bathroom, have all the things they will need ready. Run the bath and check the water for the person's preferred temperature. Have the soap, wash cloth, shampoo and other items (razor blade, cream, etc) nearby. Have the towels within easy reach. If possible, put the towels in the dryer for 2 minutes to warm them up so the person can feel warm while they are drying themselves.

Giving a Bed Bath

Bed baths may be a little (or a lot) embarrassing for people. However, they are necessary for people who cannot take a bath or shower. The person must stay clean and dry throughout the day and night. Bed baths can be quite comforting because they allow a little exercise, improve blood circulation and also provide an opportunity for gentle massage and a chat if the person would enjoy that. They also give you a chance to check for bed sores, bruises, rashes and other skin conditions. Bed baths are an intimate experience and must be done with respect and compassion. They should not be rushed. You may even want some music playing in the background for mutual enjoyment.

My father and I were very shy the first time we helped wash my mother in bed. We didn't know what we were doing so my father and I washed her from top to bottom, all at once. Then we dried her from top to bottom, all at once. She froze. We learned *wash and dry one part at a time and keep the rest covered for warmth*! She was so patient with us.

Specific Tips:

What you will need:

✓ a large bowl or basin filled with hot water (hot enough to be warming)

✓ mild soap

✓ skin lotion, cream and/or powder

✓ washcloths (for washing and rinsing) and towels

✓ personal toiletries: comb, brush, tooth brush and paste, nail file and clippers, make- up, deodorant, shaving items, perfume/cologne (whatever the person needs)

✓ a suitable change of clothes.

What you do:

✓ Wash your hands thoroughly and try and make the room temperature comfortably warm/cool, depending on the season.

✓ Let the person do as much as possible for themselves. If they cannot do much themselves:

❑ Wash one body part at a time starting at the face and working down or in the reverse direction; whichever the person prefers. The rest of the body should be covered with the top bed sheet, flannelette, or a large towel.

❑ During a bed bath, you may also put a basin of water on a towel at the foot of the bed, and help the person soak one foot at a time in the basin. It is very comforting. Towel dry the feet when they are finished.

❑ Anywhere the person's skin folds, or where they perspire most, should be washed carefully since these are the most likely spots for rashes or other skin problems. This is especially true under the arm, in the groin area, buttocks, stomach skin folds, and under a woman's breasts. In sensitive areas, the person may be able to help with the washing more than in other areas.

❑ Cleaning the back is the perfect opportunity to give someone a back rub whether they are on their stomach or on their side. Once you have cleaned them you can use skin lotion to evenly massage the upper and lower back and buttocks. Ask the person how they like their backs rubbed best and follow their lead. Use soft or harder pressure depending on what they prefer and move your hands in circular motions. Do it several times, always keeping your hands on the person's skin and using enough lotion so that your hands move smoothly.

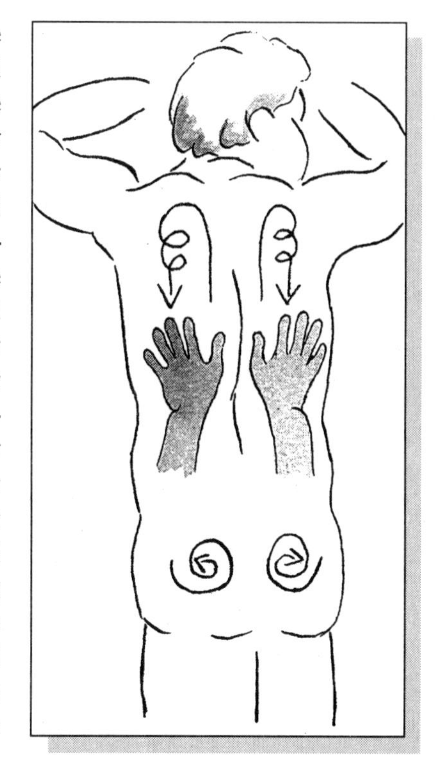

- ✓ People often enjoy having their face, temples, neck, hands, elbows, feet and heels massaged as well. Again follow their wishes.
- ✓ Once you have completely washed and dried the person, help them with their personal hygiene. For example, they may want to use deodorant, put on some makeup, have their hair combed, etc.
- ✓ Help them put on their clothes in whatever way they ask.

General Hair Care

People need their hair clean, combed/brushed (at least twice a day), cut and set. The condition of one's hair often tells visitors and the person themselves how well they are doing. Clean and groomed hair is important for good health and feeling good about yourself.

Specific Tips:

DRY SHAMPOO

You can wash someone's hair using 'dry' shampoo like a commercial dry shampoo, cornstarch or natural (unperfumed) talcum powder. This method was all the rage in the late 1960s and early 1970s for teenagers — I remember it well!

For someone who needs their hair washed in bed, dry shampoo can sometimes be a quick alternative to a normal wash. Do the following:

1. Place a towel under the person's head.
2. Sprinkle powder on the scalp and massage the hair and scalp gently.
3. Brush the powder out of the hair with slow, even strokes. If hair is tangled, hold it firmly near the scalp before brushing through to the end.
4. Wash the hairbrush after each dry shampooing.

WET SHAMPOO

If the person needs a normal hair wash but cannot use the bath or shower, you can wash their hair in bed. You will need:

- ❑ a plastic sheet to protect the bed
- ❑ a waterproof cape (like in a hair salon) or a plastic garbage bag with a hole for the head and cut along the sides to make a cape

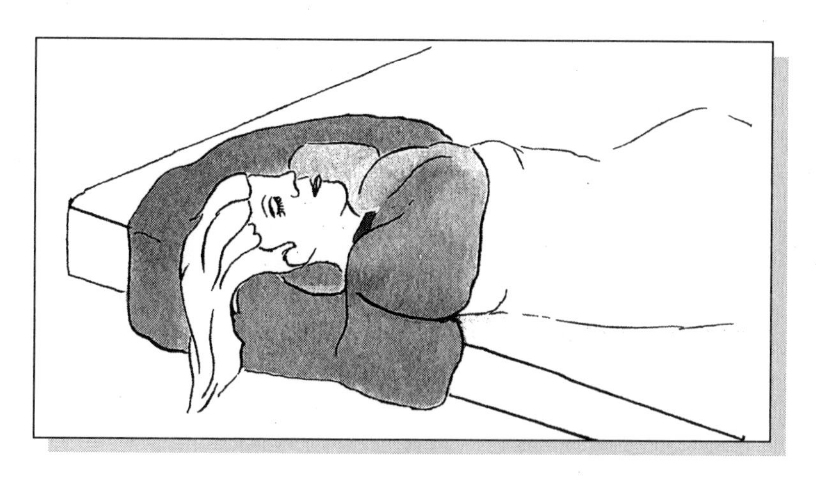

- ❑ a jug or pitcher of warm-to-hot water (several if the person has long hair)
- ❑ a bucket or large basin to collect water, (there are also special shampoo trays available through some drug stores)
- ❑ a wash cloth or small towel, plus two larger towels for drying
- ❑ pillow(s)
- ❑ shampoo
- ❑ comb or brush
- ❑ a hair dryer (if needed)

To help the person wash their hair if they are not able to do it themselves:

1. Cover the area with the plastic sheet and have the person wear their cape with the back side covering their pillow rather than tucked under them.

2. Have the person lie on their back with their head over the side of the bed (adjust pillows, covers, etc. so they are comfortable). Put the bucket or basin on a small table under the person's hair.

3. Pour warm water from the jug over their hair so that the water falls in the bucket or basin below. You may want to put a towel or plastic sheet under the bucket to catch any spill over.

4. Put shampoo onto hair and gently massage it in to lather hair and scalp.

5. Rinse hair with remaining water.

6. Dry the hair with the towel and then with the dryer if necessary.

7. Empty the bucket and tidy up the bed. Remove the cape and plastic sheet. Place a towel on the pillow to soak up any moisture still in the hair.

8. Any additional tasks like setting or coloring the hair can be done in bed using the same common sense approach to comfort and cleaning as described here.

Taking Care of Someone's Back

Many people like a back rub whether they get a bed bath or not. If the person agrees, you can give them a back rub while they lie on their stomach or on their side just as in the diagram earlier. Use a good skin lotion or experiment with natural oils such as rose or almond oil. Check with the visiting home nurse or family doctor for suggestions.

If the person cannot turn in bed themselves, they will need to be turned every two hours or so. Otherwise there will be too much pressure on just one part of their skin and they risk getting bed sores. Each time they are moved you may want to gently rub the skin where they have been laying to improve the general circulation of blood into that area. You may also want to give it a quick wash if the person has been sweating a lot. Use pillows to provide the back support they need when they are on their sides. There are some diagrams in this book that show proper pillow supports in different positions.

This may be a good point to mention that caring for someone can be quite time consuming. Just reading these instructions may be enough to make you ask if you have what it takes to do this well. When I was caring for my parents, I was a recent university graduate in the fields of history and political science. I had no experience caring for anyone (including myself if the truth is told). Using some of these basic care skills that I learned from nurses, or through trial and error, I was amazed at how calming and enjoyable they were to use on my parents. These were intimate moments of real caring. They may have been rushed sometimes, but then both they and I lost out on an experience that can remind you of what our ancestors, perhaps, knew best — physical care for people we love is one of the greatest gifts we give them and ourselves. I wouldn't have believed that if I had not experienced it.

Other Areas Needing Care

Most people will be able to brush their own teeth (or soak their dentures), clean their mouths, ears and nose. Some people may need a little bit of assistance. Let them direct you how you can best help. They may need extra help especially with their fingernails. You might brighten up a loved one's day by helping her to use her favourite nail polish.

Feet and toenails may require a good foot bath (with person sitting in chair or lying in bed with basin on a towel on the mattress). It is important to clean and dry between the toes as well as the rest of the foot. Cream or lotion will help with dryness. A good time to check and trim toe nails is after a relaxing foot soak. They should be trimmed in the same shape as their toes without sharp edges to prevent damage to other toes. The person may also enjoy a foot massage.

Adaptive Clothing

If someone must stay in bed for a long time or if they must stay around the home for long periods they may wish to adapt some of their clothes to make care easier on themselves and for others.

For example, rather than long pants or pajamas bottoms, they may wear oversized shirts or pajamas tops that are buttoned in front to keep their upper and lower body warm while also making it easier to get dressed and undressed. Sometimes, the back part of a shirt or pyjama top can get wrinkled and be quite uncomfortable for someone lying in bed for a long time. It may be worth taking some older shirts/ pyjama tops and cutting up the back and sewing a seam on each side (much like those wonderful hospital gowns everyone loves to wear). Use a strip of extra cloth to make a tie at the top and middle if you like. You can also use oversize shirts/pyjama tops and put them on backwards for a similar effect although they may not fit as nicely and may need a little cutting and sewing to fit better around the neck. Some Home Care Programs also provide hospital gowns for home use.

Scarfs (light or heavy) may be very useful to make sure that someone remains warm if there is a draft. Also scarfs can be used to keep one's head warm if the person has lost their hair during treatments. The book *Changes, Choices and Challenges* (in the reference section) gives examples of the creative uses of scarfs and cosmetics. Socks or good slippers will also help keep feet warm.

Making a Bed

People may spend a lot of time in bed. It is important that the bed stay clean, dry and comfortable.

Making an Unoccupied Bed

It seems silly to have a section on making a bed. Add to that that my mother would be amazed that I am offering advice on this subject and you get the idea that you should accept or reject any of the following advice based on your own expertise. However, many of us have never had to make a bed for someone who will spend days there. How you make the bed will decide how comfortable the person may be.

Try to use fitted bottom sheets so that the sheet has few wrinkles in it. Wrinkles add extra pressure to the person's skin and may cause bed sores. If you can, try to make the bed when the person is normally not in it (e.g. when they are taking a bath or sitting in a chair reading the morning paper). Try to avoid extra efforts to get the person out of bed just so that you can change it. The more natural the effort, the less trouble for everyone.

Making an Occupied Bed

Sometimes the person in bed cannot get out for you to change the sheets. This takes a little more planning but is quite simple after a few tries. The idea is to make one side of the bed at a time. Follow these steps:

1. Make sure you have all the clean sheets, pillow cases, etc. that you need on a chair beside the bed.
2. If possible, have the bed laying flat (if it adjustable) and the person using only one pillow.
3. Place a chair on the opposite side of the bed you are working on. If you are using a hospital bed you can raise

the far side up. Either way will allow the person in bed to hold onto something as they roll onto their side close to the chair or bed rail, their back toward you. They should be covered with a top sheet, blanket or cover so they can stay warm.

4. Loosen the bottom sheet at the head and feet end of the bed, as well as any top sheets and blankets. Roll the bottom sheet as closely to the person's back as possible. They will have to roll over this old sheet and onto the new one when you are ready.

5. Smooth out the mattress cover.

6. Lay down the clean fitted bottom sheet, folded lengthwise, from head to foot ends of the bed. Tuck in the head and foot ends and smooth out the sheet as much as possible.

7. Roll the remaining bottom sheet, lengthwise, as closely to the person's back as possible. It will be right beside the old bottom sheet.

8. Ask (or help) the person to roll toward you, over the sheets. If they need extra support, have them roll onto their back first, lift their far leg towards you gently, and help them roll onto their side facing you. Bring the chair from the other side to put where you were standing so that the person has something to hold onto and help prevent them from falling out of bed.

9. Move to the other side of the bed. Loosen the old bottom sheet and pull it completely off the bed as well as pulling the new sheet from under the person. Some of the sheets might be caught a little under the body weight of the person in bed, but just pull gently until they are loose. If necessary, gently push the bottom part of the person's back to release some of the body weight on the sheets. Smooth the mattress cover.

10. Tuck in the new bottom sheet at the head and foot end of the bed and make sure there are few, if any, wrinkles.

11. Have the person lie on their back and position the bed comfortably for them. Replace old pillow cases.

12. If the person uses a comforter, replace the outside bag as needed.

13. If the person uses sheets and blankets they will already be untucked from replacing the bottom sheets. Place a clean sheet on top of the blanket. If possible, put the new sheet in a dryer for a few minutes so it is toasty warm. Have the person hold onto the blanket and clean sheet as you pull out the old top sheet from the foot of the bed. Flip the new sheet and blanket over into the right place. If they cannot help you, you will have to do this yourself and it may take a little more time.

14. Turn the sheet and blanket around so that the blanket is on top and tuck in the top sheet and blankets (and bed spread if they like).

Extra Tips:

Sometimes there may be other things on the bottom sheet that will need to be changed or at least kept there. For example, draw sheets, sheepskin pads and incontinence pads are often used for someone who is in bed. (If possible, put the sheep's skin in the dryer on 'air' for a few minutes to fluff up the wool.) In changing the bed, the same principles apply as in the instructions above. You do one side of the bed at a time and the person needs to roll over the old and new items you are changing. The more things there are, the higher the 'bump' the person has to roll over.

Helping with Medication

The three biggest problems with taking medications (drugs) are (1) some people take far too many different ones without knowing how they react to each other, (2) they take the wrong kind of drugs or (3) they take too little of a drug for it to be helpful. For drugs to work best for you, you must have:

- ❑ the right drug
- ❑ in the right amount
- ❑ at the right time
- ❑ in the right way: liquid, tablets, drops (for ears, eyes and nose), ointment, sprays, suppositories, injections
- ❑ and working well with any other drugs you might be taking.

Whenever you see your physician, go to a clinic, or go to an emergency department, make sure to have a current list of all your medications, how often you take them and what dose you take. This will help spot any oversights in the amount and kind of medications you are taking. If you do not have a list, bring all your medications with you in the containers you got from the pharmacist.

Pharmacists are most knowledgable about drugs and their effects with other medications. When you get a prescription filled, ask the pharmacists about side effects, what will happen when you mix this prescription with other drugs (have a list of other drugs with you) and any tips they have on how to take the drugs in the right way. Also ask if there are any foods, drinks or personal habits that might affect the usefulness of the medication. For example, ask if one should not have alcohol with this medication or should not drive after taking it. Medications do affect people mentally and physically. People may have behavior changes, hallucinations or many other mild to severe reactions. You have to be very careful to make sure that medications are more helpful than harmful.

If you forget to give a drug at the right time, check with your doctor or pharmacist about what to do. Do not double the dose at the next scheduled time without their permission as this might be quite dangerous.

NOTE:
If you are taking complementary therapies like mega-dose vitamins, herbs, or are on a special diet, tell your doctor or pharmacist. For example, some Chinese herbs may be harmful when combined with medications.

Medication Records

You may be taking several drugs and it is quite common for your prescriptions to change from time to time. The following record allows you, or a family member, to keep track of your drugs, what dose you should be taking, at what time, with what conditions (e.g. take one hour before a meal, only with milk) and how well the drugs are working. The prescription date and the physician's name will be useful in emergency situations when your regular doctor is not available to help you.

Make up your own chart on some separate pages. The following is a sample of how it might look. Change it to meet your own needs.

Date	Drug	Dose	Taken	Doctor	Results/ Side Effects
Aug. 1	Tylenol 3	10 mg	4 times/day	Kildair	pain relieved after 5 hours but returned three weeks later
Aug. 23	Tylenol 3	20 mg	4 times/day	Kildair	pain relieved after 6 hours

If you are taking various drugs, a Medication Table will be very useful in helping you remember what to take, when and with what special instructions (e.g. with milk, during a meal). Use a pencil to fill in the drugs since they may change over time and you do not want to rewrite a whole schedule each time.

Time	Drug(s)	Special Instructions
8:00 a.m.	Give drug name(s) and dose.	(e.g. drug "x" with milk)
4:00 p.m.	Give drug name(s) and dose.	(e.g. do not drive after you take drug "y")
10:00 p.m.	Give drug name(s) and dose.	(e.g. at bedtime)

Make up your own schedule using the following general suggestions. Under the time column, list all the different times of the day that you will need to take drugs. Perhaps you would have 24 rows — one for each hour of the day and night.

Local pharmacies often sell "Dosettes". These boxes have many small compartments and they can be used to prepare medications for a day, or few days, at a time. They are very helpful in reminding people what to take at what time of day.

Other Pain and Symptom Control Techniques

There are other treatments for pain control. A few of these techniques use medications in a different way or use other forms of therapy such as:

1. RADIOTHERAPY: radiation is used to shrink tumors thereby reducing a person's symptoms.;
2. NERVE BLOCKS: for localized acute cancer pains, a local anesthetic or neurolytic injection is given to block nerves from sending pain messages to the brain. Results may be temporary or long-lasting.
3. HYPNOSIS: by oral suggestions a hypnotist can sometimes increase a person's pain threshold.
4. ACUPUNCTURE: this ancient Chinese art uses sterile needles in very specific spots to neutralize pain messages going to the brain.
5. NEUROSURGERY: an exacting surgery that cuts specific nerves to block them from sending pain messages to the brain. With the proper use of medication and other techniques, the need for neurosurgery should be uncommon. If other measures have failed, however, neurosurgery should not be delayed.

Total pain is not merely the sensation of pain. Total pain is a combination of physical and psychological feelings. The primary psychological component of total pain is fear. Fear can greatly aggravate a person's physical pain, so fear, anxiety and other negative emotions must also be treated. Add to this list: diarrhea, constipation, lack of hunger and energy, bed sores, lack of mobility and other symptoms and you will understand the need for symptom control and relief.

Some of the symptom control and stress management techniques that home care personnel use, other than medications, include:

1. DIET: some foods encourage constipation while others encourage loose stool. Knowing which foods cause what reaction can help caregivers to alleviate a specific symptom.

2. EXERCISE: extended bed rest can lead to bed sores, constipation, back aches, general immobility and loss of muscle strength due to decreased use of muscles. Exercises, active or passive, can be done by the person, or with someone's help, in bed or they can be done when the person is out of bed. Walking, stretching and breathing exercises are excellent forms of exercise.

3. SKIN CARE: nurses that visit homes will often tell you that bed sores are one of their greatest concerns. Bed sores are very painful and almost always avoidable. They occur most often when elbows, ankles, shoulders, hips, buttocks, heels, and the back are in constant contact with a surface. Paralyzed or unconscious people are most prone to bed sores. Proper skin care includes daily washing, skin cream treatments and the use of a lamb or sheep's skin mattress covering or water-circulating mattress pad. For people unable to move themselves in bed it is important to change their body position at least every two hours to avoid bed sores.

4. MASSAGE: gets the blood circulating, invigorates the skin and can be very soothing and or exhilarating depending on the type of massage. Everyone enjoys a massage so it is not a surprise that they are excellent for the physical and emotional well-being of many people who are ill as well.

5. OCCUPATIONAL THERAPY: recreational and physical activities within a person's physical capabilities, encourages

people to make decisions and participate in things that they have always enjoyed such as a walk in the garden or a card game with friends.

6. ART THERAPY: for the satisfaction of doing creative work and expressing feelings. Whatever the person decides to do is fine and may end up being a gift to a grandchild or a cherished memento for a family member or caregiver.

7. MUSIC THERAPY: people can relax and be comforted by playing, listening, interpreting, and talking about music. Personal preferences are paramount to the success of music therapy — just playing favourite music can be therapeutic.

8. LAUGHTER: technically it increases production of endorphins (natural chemical pain killers in our bodies), reduces tension, distracts attention, changes expectations, and is an internal jog of organs for exercise. In another sense, laughter is contagious and lets people express their feelings in a joyful way. It can change the mood of a place faster than any other emotion. Find a few good records or videos of comedians like Bill Cosby and sit back and enjoy yourself.

9. RELAXATION EXERCISES: deep breathing, visualization, hypnosis, meditation and prayer are all forms of relaxation exercises. They help to relax the body physically and mentally.

10. THERAPEUTIC TOUCH: taught in many nursing schools now, therapeutic touch involves someone moving their hands over your body, without actually touching it. The concentration and effect of this technique has been shown to reduce pain and anxiety.

11. LISTENING: perhaps no method of symptom control has a greater impact on a person's fear, anxiety, loneliness and depression than someone who will listen unconditionally and who will answer questions in an honest way.

The purpose of all of these techniques is to give people a sense of control over their lives. Even if people become bedridden, decisions have to be made about exercises, diets and other daily living tasks. These decisions force people into the decision-making process affecting their care and give them a sense of control. Independence is very important to people and symptom control helps keep them independent for as long as possible.

What Prevents Adequate Pain and Symptom Control?

Errors by the Person Receiving Care

1. believing the pain is untreatable,
2. not contacting physician for help,
3. telling physician and family that pain isn't strong,
4. failing to take medication,
5. taking medication at wrong times or inconsistently,
6. fearing addiction or drug tolerance,
7. believing pain killers are only for extreme pain,
8. discontinuing medication because of severe side effects and not telling the physician.

Physicians or Nurses' Errors

1. ignoring a person's description of pain because it sounds extreme (the pain is what the person says it is),
2. not seeing through the person's brave face,
3. prescribing pain killers that are too weak,
4. giving pain killers only when the person says the pain has returned (effective pain control prevents the return of pain),

5. believing post-operative pain killers are suitable for other kinds of pain, e.g. cancer pain (generally, surgical pain is acute but short-lasting while cancer pain is chronic and can increase over time),

6. not giving adequate information about the medication, its use and when it must/may be taken,

7. not knowing enough about different types of medication and how to move from one to another as pain increases.

To combat pain, we must recognize that pain is always real and unique for each person who has it. Proper pain control requires the right drug or treatment, in the right way, and at the right time. Proper pain control includes some experimentation to discover the right combination of medication and treatments, requiring the complete cooperation of the person, the family and the caregivers. When the pain is under control, other symptoms can be addressed, so that the person's overall suffering is reduced.

Home Care Suggestions

There are numerous books on the subject of home care and what family members can do and learn to make the situation more comfortable for everyone involved. The following are a few suggestions:

1. Remember that people do not change substantially in character because of their illness. If they were easy-going, caring and enjoyed a good joke before their illness they will probably be the same now. If they were unsatisfied with their lives, not easy to please and don't like to talk much, they will probably not change a great deal because they are ill or stuck at home. Therefore, treat them respectfully and give them the opportunity to direct your involvement in their care.

2. Do not try to force someone to eat. People need control over their lives and should be encouraged to make their own decisions. People know that food is important to living. Their diet may be prescribed but a hot plate, small cooler or refrigerator by the bed will permit them to eat many small meals when they are hungry. Also have lots of liquids readily available. If the person needs some help with eating, remember to keep common courtesies as part of the help. Do not make them go too fast or too slow. Give them a proper napkin and place setting, if possible. Remember that older people's tongues change shape and they must be fed differently than young children or adults.

3. Daily baths or washing, massages and general hygiene are critical for comfort but also to prevent bed sores for bedridden people. Bed sores are very painful and almost always avoidable.

4. If conditions permit, encourage people to decide if they wish to smoke, drink, walk around, and have visitors. Even if these activities are tiring or unhealthy, the decision must rest with the person who is ill, unless it harms someone else.

5. Although family members often want to do what is best for their loved one, they must not forget about themselves. If you feel like you are being used, say so. If you are uncomfortable with decisions that the ill person has made, be honest about your feelings and arrange for someone else to help.

6. Have a bedside bell, voice monitor or other device available so that people in bed feel they have direct access to you. An ability to make contact, at their discretion, is crucial for the emotional support of people who are ill.

7. Have music and television available should the person choose to listen or watch. People who are great sports fans, for example, may benefit from some cable television that runs sports most of the day. This may be a great distraction from what is happening to them physically.

8. Plastic bed pans, vomit trays, basins and the like are not as cold as metal ones.

9. For the caregivers at home, get all the assistance you need from your family, friends and professionals. Most people do not know what to do under these circumstances so they need to know how they can be helpful at this important time.

10. If the person is chronically or terminally ill you may want to buy or borrow a home care book which gives you even further suggestions about how to care for the person at home. (See General Reference List at the back of this book for some suggestions.)

Good Nutrition

It makes sense that what goes into a body affects how well a body heals itself or comforts itself. Good eating habits and good nutrition can make a world of difference to how one feels and how one heals. The book, **What to Eat When You Don't Feel Like Eating**, *(listed at the back of this book) is an excellent, short cookbook of healing recipes for all people, but especially those who are sick. You must also remember how important it is to keep drinking throughout the day so that you do not become dehydrated during an illness.*

Some things to keep in mind about healthier and more enjoyable eating (these are in no particular order):

1. We all have different nutritional needs, tastes and appetites. When anyone is ill, the needs may have to be adapted to what the person can tolerate or even enjoy. Some children, for example, may not be able to eat very much but they might have something from their favorite fast food restaurant. It may not be perfect but it is a beginning.

2. Someone's appetite depends on their physical condition, level of exercise and other distractions. Someone with little to do but watch television may begin to eat larger amounts of unhealthy food that they normally would not eat.

3. Medications, poor teeth, chronic fatigue and one's overall condition may affect their appetite and taste buds. Simple oral hygiene can improve one's joy of food so encouraging regular brushing is still important when someone is ill or recovering from a condition.

4. A well-balanced diet includes food from different food groups:

PROTEINS from fish, poultry, meat, eggs;
MILK AND MILK PRODUCTS;
FRUITS AND VEGETABLES and
WHOLE-GRAIN BREADS AND CEREALS.
From a good combination of these groups, one gets the nutrition, vitamins and minerals necessary for healthier living.

5. People need varying quantities of food. They may need more from one food group than the others depending on their condition. Some people need to eat less and healthier to regain strength. Athletes require more bulk foods from whole-grain breads, pasta and cereals. People weaken from too little food over a long period of recovery need to eat higher calorie meals. *It is necessary to speak with a nutritionist, dietician or other knowledgeable person about what foods, and in what quantities, the person who is ill or recovering should eat.* People should be able to eat what they enjoy as well as what is 'good for them'. A balanced diet allows for sweats, snacks and desserts in moderation. People may also enjoy something completely new since they will have no memory of this new food ever affecting them badly like their more familiar foods.

6. Serving meals should, when possible, include meals that are not all the same color (e.g. all yellow vegetables, white potatoes, apple sauce and pale meat). Making the meal visually pleasing may encourage a healthier appetite. Dishes, the food tray and napkins should be clean. The food tray should rest comfortably on the person's lap or on a small bed tray.

7. Some people prefer, or need, smaller meals offered more often than the standard three meals a day. For example, someone might benefit from smaller portions of food every 2-3 hours with snacks by the bedside during the night. It is better to offer less, than too much. Too large a portion can be overwhelming and, literally, nauseating.

8. Any little memorable thing you can do to add to the joy of a meal is a gift. For example, bringing the morning paper with breakfast, having a flower on the tray with lunch, or giving a puzzle for a child to play with after dinner.

9. Eating is often a social gathering. The person who is in bed may truly enjoy the company of others with them as they eat rather than eating alone. Conversation, review of everyone's day and general social activity may encourage someone to eat more than they had originally thought they could.

10. People often have very particular habits around their meals. These should be followed as much as possible. For example, if someone likes to 'dress for dinner', help them with any grooming concerns and bed clothes you can. If they enjoy some background music, try to make this available in their room. If they generally carve the meat, try to accommodate this tradition.

11. Help people wash their hands before and after a meal.

12. If the person can come to the dining table, encourage them to do so. If they need to stay in their room, you might set up a card table or other temporary table there. If the person needs to remain in bed, make sure their back is well supported with pillows while they are in the sitting position.

13. If the person requires assistance with cutting their meal and/or with feeding, remember they are not a baby and, therefore, should be helped in the most respectful and relaxed way possible. The person should continue to feel as a valued member of the family rather than a patient dependent on aid to eat. Follow the person's lead as best as possible so you are helping them in ways that are most supportive.

14. When helping someone to eat, the food should be bite size, spoons should only be filled two-thirds full, and the pace should be leisurely. Clear the tray away as soon as the meal is finished and then spend a little extra time, if they want, socializing before dishes are done. Straws can be very helpful.

15. The room where the person is eating should be at a comfortable temperature, tidied with as much fresh air as is comfortable. The food and drink should be the right temperature for the person. Warn the person if any food or drink is very hot.

16. Check to see if it is possible for the person to have their usual wine, coffee or other drinks with their meals.

Family and Friends:

Visiting Someone Who is Ill or Recovering

Many family members and friends find it difficult to visit someone who is ill. If the person is at home, it may be more difficult for some family members and friends to overcome their fear and visit because they may think it is less important than visiting someone in hospital.

It is natural to hesitate in seeing someone you love who is recovering from an illness or who is seriously ill. Here are some suggestions that may help you to visit them:

1. If you care about the person then go and visit, even if you are not great friends (e.g. a colleague from work).

2. Check with the person or family to see when the best time would be to visit. You don't want 20 people arriving one day and no one coming the next.

3. Remember that the person you love has not changed. They may be your parent, your child or a dear friend. Their personality, the qualities you admire and love, have not changed because they are ill or tired. Respect them rather than baby them. Include them in decisions. Ask their advice. They will probably change less than you will.

4. There is nothing as comforting as a touch. If the person will allow you and if you feel comfortable yourself, sit close to the person, hold their hand and give them a hug. Your touch and the caring in your eyes express more than words ever can.

5. Use open-ended questions to permit the person to decide what they want to talk about (if they want to talk at all). Questions like: "How are you feeling today?" "How can I help you be more comfortable?" "I love you so much. Is there anything I can do or say that would help?"

6. Perhaps you can show or give this book to a family member or a friend to help them understand better what is happening to them and to the people around them. A small section of the book may open up the discussion in a non-threatening way. A book like this left with a person may, or may not, be read but it provides information to people who are naturally curious.

7. Don't prepare a speech. Admit your fear of illness or sick people. The person needs to feel useful and if you are honest they can help you overcome some of your fear so that you can have a really good talk.

8. Be yourself. Act as you always do with the person. If you are naturally quiet then avoid telling all the latest jokes from work. If you normally gossip about old friends then continue to do so. If you are naturally outgoing don't become sombre and serious. People need stability in their lives and family and friends can offer the greatest emotional stability.

9. Let the person vent their anger, frustration and despair. Their feelings are real and they need to get them out. It may have nothing to do with their illness but could be their treatment, their employer's attitude, old friends who no longer visit, or an acquaintance who owes them money but is nowhere to be seen. Offer to help if you can help improve their situation.

10. It is often not helpful to compare the person with other people who have gone through similar things. It minimizes their own feelings.

11. It is all right to cry and show your own feelings. You don't have to be strong all the time, for that makes the person dependent on your strength. If you cry and allow them to be strong it is a normal relationship and one that benefits both of you.

12. Don't hide behind a gift or card for it is your presence that is the gift. You can send a card or gift if you are unable to visit, or between visits, to let the person know you are thinking of her.

13. Try not to stay too long. Two short visits are better than one long one. This is especially true if the person tires easily.

14. Remember the other family members. They need your emotional support, too, and practical things like transportation, food, baby-sitting and running errands can reduce their stress and provide them with the precious gift of time.

Talking with Your Doctor and other Caregivers

Understanding the Physician and Other Professional Caregivers

There is a natural apprehension by many people toward anything medical. In the past few years, however, there has been a heightened awareness that everyone benefits when the person and family work together with their professional caregivers. Open and honest communication relieves the person and family's anxiety, while the physicians and caregivers feel more job satisfaction and less personal stress.

Caregivers endure stresses that everyone can help diminish by working together. For example, the professional stresses of many professional caregivers include:

1. heavy workload (it isn't enough to be a health care provider these days; you must also be a business person, a politician, and a bureaucrat);
2. deciding how much people should know about their illness (although most people prefer to know the truth about their illness, there are those who prefer that the physician not tell them the complete truth);
3. the increasing administrative requirements of governments and insurance companies;
4. little time to learn new treatments and methods even though some professionals (e.g. physicians) must study a certain number of hours per year to keep their license;
5. little time for personal stress reduction;
6. increasing numbers of lawsuits; and
7. a decreased public respect for the medical professionals in general.

Understanding People Who are Ill, and Their Families

Quality total care looks at the physical, emotional, spiritual and informational needs of the person who is ill and their family members. Studies show that many people who are ill want the same things, including:

1. to be relatively pain free;
2. to be alert and aware of what is happening to them;
3. to have the companionship of their family and friends;
4. to be accepted as the person they have always been;
5. to maintain their individuality;
6. not to be a burden to their family and caregivers;
7. to have familiar things around them: photos, plants, music, flowers, favorite food, pets;
8. to be cared for and remembered with love and respect;
9. to have their family get the support they need to help the person stay at home;
10. to have enough information to make informed choices about their treatment and care.

People who are ill and their families must accept responsibility for encouraging improved communication with their professional caregivers because the consequences of an uncooperative relationship affects the person and family most directly. This is not always easy because some people have a real fear of anything medical, they may have an uncooperative caregiver or they may have family problems that prevent good communication.

Of course some communication problems between someone who is ill and their professional caregivers arise because the person has few family or friends to support them during discussions with professionals. They may have outlived their spouse or partner, their children may not live nearby or they may be isolated because of a lack of services for our growing numbers of elders. They can be quite overwhelmed with the well-meaning care of a diverse group of professionals with little support to make sense of their condition, their needs or their personal care at home. These people may fall through the cracks of our health care and Home Care Programs. Extra diligence on the part of professionals within health care facilities and Home Care Programs is necessary to help these people find more natural supports within their communities.

Some Tips

From the physician and other caregivers' points of view there are proven techniques that people can use to improve the patient-caregiver relationship.

Some Do's:

Some people will choose not to try the following suggestions and, in effect, choose not to communicate and cooperate. Whether we agree with their decisions or not, it is their decision and they must be respected (unless they injure someone else).

1. Know your caregivers' names and help them remember yours.
2. Communicate with them about your physical, emotional, spiritual and informational needs.
3. Cooperate fully once a decision on treatment is mutually decided.
4. Write down the important questions to ask (usually in groups of three) and record the caregiver's answers (or bring a loved one along and let them record the answers).
5. Respect the caregiver's time while expecting the same in return.

6. Ask concise questions rather than ""Why did this happen to me?"

7. Offer a time limit for discussion (e.g. 8 minutes) and stick to it. In this way you build up a trusting relationship with the caregivers and they know you respect their time.

Some Don'ts:

Some don'ts include:

1. Ignore medical instructions after a mutual medical decision has been made;

2. ask too many questions, over and over again, (it is better to record the physician's answers);

3. bring up questions about other family members and friends in hope of free medical advice;

4. keep telephoning with questions to one caregiver that can be better answered by other experts such as a nurse, pharmacist or therapist;

5. wait to communicate new pains or negative symptoms until they have become serious;

6. forget to communicate emotional needs rather than putting on a brave face;

7. get a second medical opinion without first telling the principal physician;

8. follow other medical or alternative therapies without consulting the principal physician because the different therapies may conflict;

9. forget to treat the caregivers with respect or concern.

Resolving Communication Problems

When open communication does not seem possible, there are other options available. When the problem has become serious, bring in a community or hospital social worker or the discharge planner/Home Care Case Manager to see if improvements can be made. Other caregivers such as a cleric, nurse, or psychologist may also be helpful.

Where the communication cannot be improved, the person and family can do one or both of the following (although I recognize that during such an emotional time these suggestions will not be easy to follow):

1. change specialists on the advice of your family physician or another caregiver;
2. change hospitals or the service you are using.

If it is the person or family that is uncooperative, the physician might recommend a different physician or hospital. The doctor must legally continue care until the person has found a new physician.

Many communication problems are not always one person's fault. People have different personalities and for whatever reason, some people do not communicate well with each other. If both people recognize the problem and accept the situation, the caregiver can help find someone to replace him.

In the case of family members, a physician may find it easier to speak to a single member of the family rather than the whole family. Recognizing that the person who is ill is the physician's paramount concern, the family can arrange to choose a member to act as spokesperson and minimize the time a physician needs to spend with the whole family. This spokesperson should still have one other person with them to help listen and record answers to important questions.

After all the studies have been read, the personal experiences related, and the advice given, the underlying principle of total care of the person who is ill or recovering remains *co-operation between the person, family and caregiver.* A mutual respect and understanding of each others' feelings and needs will result in a fuller life for the person who is ill and a personal satisfaction for the family members and caregivers that they have helped the person to the best of their abilities.

Understanding Your Condition

Questions Caregivers Need Answered

You will probably see many doctors, nurses, pharmacists and other caregivers during the length of your illness, condition or recovery. They all want many of the same answers to the following questions. If you have prepared them in writing in advance it can save you some time.

1. What specifically concerns you about your condition today?
2. What is the history of this condition?
3. Where in the body did the pain/symptom begin?
4. When did it start (date and time)?
5. On a scale of 1-10 with 10 equalling the worst pain you have ever had (i.e. broken arm, appendicitis) how would you measure your pain?
6. Describe any other symptoms you have had?
7. What were you doing at the time of the pain/symptom?
8. To what degree does your pain/symptom limit your normal activities?
9. How long does the pain/symptom last? (an hour, all day)
10. Is the pain/symptom constant or does it change?
11. Does the pain/symptom stay in one place or spread out to other parts of your body?
12. What makes the pain/symptom worse?
13. What makes the pain/symptom better?
14. How do the following things affect your symptoms: bowel

movements, urination, coughing, sneezing, breathing, swallowing, menstruation, exercise, walking, and eating?

15. What do you intuitively feel is wrong?

16. Do you have any other information that might help me?

Your Questions about Tests

Even though you are at home now, you may need to return to a hospital or clinic for further tests and treatments. The following questions will help you to understand your condition and have some control over what happens to you. That control will probably help you recover at home faster.

Studies have shown that people who are aware of the physical effects of a test or treatment are less afraid and recover more quickly from a difficult procedure than people with little or no advanced information. Although caregivers may not have had a particular test themselves, they can usually provide fairly detailed information based on other peoples' experiences and the medical literature on the specific test or treatment. It is important for a person to understand why a physician has recommended a test and how the test is done. The following questions can be asked of a physician, nurse or technician to help the person decide whether or not they will consent to the test.

1. What is the purpose of this/these tests?

2. What do you expect to learn from these tests? Will the results change my treatment in any way?

3. What will the test feel like (any pain or discomfort)?

4. What are the common risks involved in these tests?

5. Are there any side effects to these tests?

6. Can I be accompanied by my spouse/child/friend? If not, why not? (The medical world is slowly changing to permit someone to be with the person through difficult tests. The change toward this system is similar to how fathers are now finally allowed into delivery rooms.)

7. Can I return home after the test?
8. When will I get the results of these tests? Can I see you to go over them with you?
9. What will happen to me if I choose not to take these tests?
10. What are the chances of error or false positive/negative results? (Some tests have a high incidence of "false positives". Often tests cannot be definitive but they can help physicians know if they are on the right track.)
11. What are the costs involved, if any?
12. [Other questions specific to your illness or condition?]

Your Questions about Drugs

You may ask the following questions of your pharmacist or physician. Some of the information, however, will be listed on the medication or included with the medication. People are responsible for thinking about these questions whenever they are asked to take new medication. Keep in mind that people react in different ways to medications while others do not follow instructions carefully enough.

Some of the answers to the following questions can be found in any of the standard pharmaceutical books listed at the back of this book. If your pharmacist or physician cannot answer your questions with sufficient detail, check with one of the reference texts.

1. What is the name and purpose of these drugs?
2. What do the drugs actually do inside my body?

3. How often do I take them each day and for how many days?

4. What food, liquids, activities and other medications should I avoid when taking these drugs?

5. What are the effects of mixing these various drugs together?

6. What are the common and less common side effects of these drugs?

7. How can these side effects be controlled?

8. When should I return to give you feedback about the effectiveness of the drugs?

9. What will happen if I chose not to take these drugs?

10. What are some alternatives to taking drugs for my condition?

11. Is there a less expensive generic version of these drugs?

12. What special storage instructions should I follow? (Pharmacists usually label medication with specific instructions but you should ask if the labels are not clear.)

13. Can this prescription be repeated without coming to see you again?

14. What are the costs involved? (Many prescriptions are never filled because people do not tell their physicians that they cannot afford the medication.)

15. Do you know if my medical insurance covers any of these costs? (Ask your insurance agent or government insurance official this question.)

16. What reactions can I expect by taking this drug along with the other drugs I already take? (List other drugs)

17. [Other questions specific to your illness or condition?]

Questions to Your Physicians about Your Condition

Once you have been physically examined and appropriate tests are done, you will talk with your physician about your condition. Your family physician, as your advocate and mediator in the medical world, should help you understand the medical system. Why and how are tests done? What does the diagnosis of your condition mean to you? What treatment alternatives are there? What is the prognosis (prediction of the probable course of a disease) for your condition? What types of support (financial, physical, emotional, spiritual and informational) are available to you?

Try to get your family physician actively involved if you have difficulty understanding or communicating with your specialists. Always make sure that you understand what your physicians are saying. It is common for them to use terms you may not understand. Physicians have had to learn what these terms mean, so they can discuss them with you and help you understand them too.

In order not to waste your physician's time, it is important to ask specific questions. You might give your physician a copy of the following checklist of items which you would like answered, especially if your situation has changed dramatically since your last visit.

Fill in the answers to your questions so you do not have to repeat the questions at a later point. Even better, have someone with you (family member, friend) to take notes for you so you can concentrate on the discussion with your physician. Also ask for reference material that might answer some of the questions for you. This will greatly reduce the time commitment of your physician and allow you to return later with even more specific questions and concerns. There will be times, of course, when your physician cannot give you specific answers because your disease may not be predictable. However, your physician can offer some educated guesses with recommendations of where you can go to get further information.

I. DIAGNOSIS

Diagnosis is not always an exacting science because there are many unknown variables. This is why second opinions are sometimes necessary. Physicians can usually provide an accurate diagnoses with those illnesses and conditions that have exacting scientific tests to confirm a diagnosis. One must be careful, however, that the test was done accurately and that the conclusions are confirmed in serious conditions before making major treatment decisions.

1. What do I have?
2. How did I get it?
3. How can I prevent it from happening again or getting worse?
4. [Other questions specific to your illness or condition?]

II. THE DISEASE ITSELF

1. Based on your experience and the medical literature, what is the usual progress of this disease?
2. What can I expect next?
3. What other parts of my physical and mental abilities will be affected?
4. [Other questions specific to your illness or condition?]

III. INFECTIONS

1. Can I give this illness to others and if I can, how would they get it from me (physical contact, through the air)?
2. [Other questions specific to your illness or condition?]

IV. OTHER POSSIBLE DISEASES

1. Could the test results and symptoms indicate a different disease than the one you mention?

2. [Other questions specific to your illness or condition?]

V. TREATMENT

1. What treatment do you suggest?

2. How does the treatment work?

3. How will I be able to evaluate its success or failure?

4. How long after I begin the treatment should I see you again to report any progress?

5. How often will I need the treatment?

6. What are the side effects to this treatment?

7. What are some of the medical and non-medical alternatives of these treatments?

8. [Other questions specific to your illness or condition?]

VI. PROGNOSIS

Prognosis is a prediction of the probable course and outcome of a disease or condition. It is not an exacting science. While you want to know what is probably going to happen to you, there are many variables which may give you a different outcome than what is expected in other people. Your body, mind and spirit are unique and what happens to you may be very different than what happens to other people.

1. What is the expected outcome of this illness?

2. What will happen if I choose not to treat this illness through medication, surgery or other treatments?

3. What are the long-term effects of this illness?

4. Will I have pain as the disease develops?

5. [If the condition is very serious you might ask]: What is an educated guess as to how long I have to live?

6. [Other questions specific to your illness or condition?]

Questions When You Go To a Hospital

When you go to a hospital, it is important to remember that you are there to receive a service. You remain in control of that service by consenting to, or refusing, the tests and treatments offered to you. You can refuse any and all treatments and tests offered you if you wish.

1. If English is not your first language, ask if there is anyone who can speak to you in your own language and help you understand your medical care.

2. What is the name of the admitting physician?

3. Who is the physician in charge of my case and how can I reach him or her? Who is the Nurse Manager of this unit and how can I reach her or him?

4. Is the physician in charge of my case a specialist, intern, resident or medical student?

5. What special rules and regulations should I be aware of while I am in this facility?

6. What is the discharge procedure for leaving this facility?

7. Is this a teaching hospital, and if it is, will anyone be requesting that I participate in any research or educational program? (You have the right to consent or refuse to be part of any research or educational program.)

8. Does the hospital have a patient advocate office or social worker who can answer any of my questions regarding hospital procedures?

9. What costs are involved in my hospital stay, if any?

10. [Other questions specific to your illness or condition?]

Questions before Surgery

Surgery is a frightening proposition for most people. If people understand the reasons for surgery, the procedures that will be followed and the results they can expect, then their fear and anxiety is greatly reduced. Again, studies have shown that people who understand what is happening to them will recover more quickly and often feel less pain because of reduced anxiety.

1. What are the benefits and risks to this surgery?
2. What are the alternatives, their benefits and risks?
3. What is the prognosis if I choose not to have surgery?
4. What are the risks of anaesthesia in my condition? When will the Anesthesiologist meet with me to explain the procedures?
5. What is the success rate for this surgery?
6. What are the pre-surgery procedures?
7. What happens during the actual surgery?
8. What are the post-surgery procedures?
9. Will I have much pain and discomfort after surgery?
10. What things can I expect to see so that I am not worried when I wake up, e.g. will I be on a respirator, will I have blood transfusions, and will I be in the intensive care unit?
11. What is the expected length for my recovery from surgery?
12. How soon after surgery can I go to the bathroom, eat, walk, go home, go to work, have sex, smoke and drink alcohol?
13. What are the names of the surgeons who will be operating?

14. Will there be any medical students operating? (You have the option to refuse treatment by anyone other than your surgeon.)

15. What are the costs involved, if any?

16. [Other questions specific to your illness or condition?]

Creating Your Own Support Team

June Callwood's book *Twelve Weeks in Spring* tells the story of Margaret Frazer. In 1985 Margaret was dying of cancer and did not want to go into hospital or become involved in a formal palliative care program. June Callwood and other friends recruited close to 60 friends, acquaintances from Margaret's volunteer work, church, and other volunteers to help her stay at home until her death. They each provided practical help as well as physical and emotional comforts a few hours per week. Margaret's doctor was part of this "support team" and provided the others with information to help Margaret stay as comfortable as possible. Near the end of Margaret's life, this support team provided round-the-clock care and support.

From that experience several of Margaret's friends from the church of the Holy Trinity in Toronto and other volunteers established Trinity Hospice Toronto to help people who wanted to keep as much control over their lives as possible through an informal hospice program. The volunteers at Trinity Hospice Toronto (now called Trinity Home Hospice) provide practical care and supports during 1-3 hour visits with someone who has a terminal or life-threatening illness. These volunteers are not trained medical staff (although some volunteers have professional backgrounds) nor is their purpose to replace home care and homemaker supports available through government health care. Their purpose is to provide the kind of practical help and emotional support that friends and good neighbours have been providing to each other for generations.

What these people learned and practiced can be used by anyone who needs to stay at home for a long time. It is not limited to people who have a life-threatening illness. It can easily be used for someone who has a chronic illness; for someone (old or young) who lives at home alone and needs some extra help to stay in their own home rather than move in with family or into an institution; for a parent who would like some time away from the children once or twice a week; and for people who would like to increase their circle of friends. In other words, do not be limited by the ideas presented here. Let your imagination run wild with potential rather than with limitations.

I spoke with Trinity Hospice Toronto's Co-ordinator (Bev Pelton) and Resource Person (Elaine Hall) in 1993 about how people could design their own support teams to allow them the most control and flexibility. Not everyone wants to receive care through a formal program and others do not have formal care programs available to them where they live. Developing a support team is one alternative. You may also want to check if your area has volunteer programs to help people stay at home rather than go to the hospital or long-term care facility. They may provide you with more information and, perhaps, volunteer support.

The following ideas are not in any specific order. You might use some or all of the following ideas to develop a support team. Take only those ideas that apply to you and change or add ideas that meet the specific needs of the person needing care. Remember that a support team is only effective when the person needing care agrees with the idea and is an active participant in the decision making.

Throughout the ideas presented here I will use the word friends to include family members and friends who do not live with the person who is ill, as well as volunteers who over time may become friends of the person.

1. It helps to have one or two friends act as the co-ordinator(s) of the support team. This person is generally not the closest loved one (partner, parent or adult child). The co-ordinator is responsible for organizing everyone's schedule for visiting the person who is at home. Freeing this responsibility from the closest loved one allows that person to concentrate on the person who is ill and vice versa rather than concentrating on the day-to-day details of scheduling and answering phone calls. It also gives the person and loved ones more time to relax, go out for walks, eat together quietly, and make plans for themselves and their family.

2. How do you recruit enough friends? The co-ordinator can ask other family, friends and work colleagues who live in the area; people from clubs and organizations that the person belongs to (e.g. Rotary, volunteer work, veterans groups), and churches/synagogues/temples where the person worships for help in visiting the person. Another group that is often overlooked are neighbours. Neighbours are often willing to drop by with some food, helping run some errands, keeping up the yard, shovelling snow, or popping in early in the morning or late at night to help the person get in or out of bed. *Since the co-ordinator is not the person who needs care or a member of the immediate family, people will feel more comfortable saying no if they do not want to participate.*

3. The number of friends one person might need depends completely on the needs of the person staying at home and how many different people they would like coming to their home. *Some people only want and need the help of a few familiar people.* Other people may need more help, especially if their condition requires round-the-clock physical care. Trinity Home Hospice often schedules people into three-hour visits once every week or every two weeks if there are enough people. A general schedule they follow is:

9 p.m. - 8 a.m. (night visit if possible and necessary)
8 a.m. - 12 p.m.
12 p.m. - 3 p.m.
3 p.m. - 6 p.m.
6 p.m. - 9 p.m.

They suggest that if there are overnight visits the friend brings their own linen and a change of clothes so that they can leave directly from the person's home to go to work or back to their own home ready to start the day.

If this schedule is necessary to provide adequate support it would require five people per day (other than any immediate family that lives with the person) or 35 people per week. Some people may want to volunteer more than one shift a week and this would certainly cut down on the number of people required.

Except for the night person, everyone commits to only a three-hour visit once a week. It sounds like a lot of people. It is. However, if you quickly review you list of friends and neighbors, you will easily find several dozen who would be keen to help a few times a week. When I was caring for my parents there were only two or three of us doing all of the round-the-clock work. In hindsight, if we had accepted the help of only a few people, we would have all done considerably better physically, emotionally and spiritually.

It is helpful for everyone on the team to have the monthly schedule and a list of all team members and their telephone numbers. Encourage team members to find their own replacements if they cannot make an appointment and let the co-ordinator know about any changes to the schedule.

4. As well as visiting the person at home, friends often meet once a month, or more often depending on the illness, to compare notes and feelings. Often the person receiving support participates in these meetings if they want or they may ask one of their family members to go. These meetings can be held in the person's home or elsewhere depending on the person's wishes and the space available.

5. What qualifications must a friend have? A friend is there to provide emotional and spiritual support, practical help, companionship and to lessen the fear and isolation of the person who is ill and their family. Trinity Home Hospice states some of the qualifications as follows: motivated to help without interfering; emotional maturity; tolerance for different social cultural and religious beliefs; warmth, empathy, tact and discretion; flexibility; dependability; good listening skills; ability to work with others as a team member; different talents and skills (e.g. from past work experiences and hobbies); and a sense of humour (it is helpful not to take yourself too seriously). The key is to be there for the person and not to be there to fulfil your own, unspoken needs — to provide unconditional support and compassion.

6. Trinity Home Hospice recommends that the person uses the services offered through the Home Care Program and homemaking services where available. These services will depend on the area you live in and may include: visits by nurses, physio/occupational therapists, social workers, dieticians, homemaker help (e.g. to cook some meals, do dishes, do shopping and some light cleaning); as well as home chemotherapy treatments and other intravenous therapies, nutrition counselling and overnight nursing. The Home Care Case Manager can help you identify all the services available where you live.

7. A communication log book is a helpful tool when more than a few people are involved in providing support at home. In this log book, friends, volunteers, professional caregivers (family doctor, visiting nurses) and family members can write notes about the likes and dislikes of the person, information that needs to be passed on to different people who will visit later that day or week, etc. The person often reads the comments and adds comments of their own. Some people who are ill or recovering like the idea of a log book and others do not, so check before hand. The book may also include information about what to do in an emergency, the person's provincial health care number, next of kin, medications, name and number of co-ordinator, and name and number of family physician. If for some reason the person needed to go to hospital the log book could be taken to provide up-to-date information.

8. Recognize that not everyone who wants to help the person will be appreciated, for various reasons. If the person who is ill prefers not to have someone come to their home, the co-ordinator would tell the friend or volunteer that the person's wishes are paramount and should not be taken personally. Some people just do not "click" and that is perfectly acceptable. That person might still participate by cooking some meals, answering phones, or running errands,

9. Recognize that whenever a few people get together there will be tensions, misunderstandings and mistakes. People are doing their best but they may do little things that annoy one another. Recognize these stresses and discuss them with others on a one-to-one basis or at general meetings if the problem goes beyond a few people. A example would be people who enter the person's home without taking off their shoes. This custom is perfectly acceptable in most people's homes but unacceptable in other people's homes. Knowing these little things will help make the experience more positive for everyone. The key is to remember that you are visiting someone's home where they are used to certain routines and behaviors. It is quite different from visiting that person in a hospital where their routines must blend in with the hospital's methods and expectations.

10. It is sometimes difficult to draw the line between providing support and making decisions for the person. We all have opinions and feelings about what the right way to do something is. For example, some people would like to be alone while others would like to have many people nearby. Regardless of your views and wishes, you must, as a friend, follow the wishes of the person as best you can. If you strongly disagree with a decision the person makes (on ethical or personal grounds) try to get another friend to be with the person. Call the co-ordinator to make different arrangements so that you do not have to do something against your strongly held beliefs and that the person does not have to give up control over their live in order to make you happy. This line between providing support and making decisions for a person should be discussed at most general meetings to help remind people of this gentle, yet vital, balance.

11. If the person requires care for a long time, there will be friends who will come and go because of other commitments. When new people come it is difficult at first for them to fit into what has probably become a tightly-knit group. For the person, who may be more ill than when the team began, it is one more person coming into their life and home. Recognize some of the difficulties and provide extra support to both the person getting support and the new visitor.

12. Friends will hear confidential information from the person and their family members. All this information is confidential and must not be repeated to anyone without permission. This includes telling one's own family and curious neighbours what is happening behind closed doors.

13. Use the talents you have rather than trying to learn many new ones. Find people who have the skills and interests you miss so that you can concentrate on giving that part of yourself to someone else that you are both most comfortable with. For example, you may enjoy reading and writing and could help the person with their mail or reading a book with them. Someone else may help without necessarily being with the person who is ill. They may enjoy cooking, cleaning, gardening, walking the dog, or running errands without having to spend time with the person. Other people may enjoy helping the person eat their food, doing arts and crafts together, or doing bookkeeping, financial or legal matters together (or alone).

"Being there" is also a wonderful gift. Sometimes people don't want to talk, listen or do things. They want to rest, think, pray or day dream. Being there means that you do not interrupt but give them the privacy or companionship the person wants.

14. People who have a cold, flu or infection should not visit the person until they feel better themselves. You would not want to pass on the illness to the person.

Spending time with someone who is ill or needs to stay at home for a long time is very rewarding and can also be traumatic. Friends must take care of themselves and each other. People need time to think about what they are experiencing and to talk about their experiences, joys, sadness and frustrations. Take the time and make the efforts. Having helped my parents and my grandfather live at home until they died are some of my richest experiences. I learned so much about them and so much about myself. I took the time to try to understand what I was thinking and feeling. There were many happy moments and some sad ones. The wealth of that experience will sustain me for the rest of my life. Enjoy the learning. Enjoy the giving. Enjoy the receiving.

For further information on care support teams write or call ***Trinity Home Hospice***: P.O. Box 324, Commerce Court Postal Station, Toronto, Ontario, M5L 1G3, Canada — (416) 364-1666 or FAX (416) 364-2231. You may also want to check you telephone book to see if there is a Citizen Advocacy group in your area. Citizen Advocacy groups have extensive experience helping people who are ill, disabled, vulnerable or marginalized by bringing together community members who want to help others in practical and compassionate ways as friends. ***Toronto Citizen Advocacy*** can be reached at 73 Simcoe Street, 2nd Floor, Toronto, Ontario, M5J 1W9; 416-597-1131. ***The Canadian Palliative Care Association*** keeps an up-to-date list of palliative/hospice care groups across the country. They can be reached at 5 Blackburn Avenue, Ottawa, Ontario, K1N 8A2; 800-668-2785. If you are not in touch with your local HOME CARE Program, you may want to find out what services they offer. Many disease or condition-specific organizations also provide different kinds of supports (e.g. cancer societies, Red Cross, meals on wheels, friendly visiting services, community agencies, and private home care agencies).

Glossary

The following list includes medical definitions, descriptions of various medical specialists, and common abbreviations used on medical charts and prescriptions. For a complete definition use a more extensive standard medical dictionary.

Abscess A sac of pus formed by the breakdown of infected or inflamed tissue.

a.c. abbrev. = before meals.

Acupressure A method of pain relief using finger pressure on the same points used in acupuncture.

Acupuncture Chinese medical practice of using needles inserted through the skin in specific points to restore the balance of a body's energy flow.

Acute Condition with symptoms that develop quickly, are severe, but do not last long. Opposite to chronic condition.

Addiction Uncontrollable craving for a substance with an increasing tolerance and physical dependence on it.

Allergist Often an Internist who also specializes in the treatments of allergies.

Allergy A reaction to environmental factors or substances which may cause a rash, swelling or more serious physical response.

Alopecia Temporary or permanent loss of hair (may occur as a side-effect of chemotherapy).

Amyotrophic Lateral Sclerosis (Lou Gerhig's Disease) A deterioration of the spinal cord resulting in the wasting away of muscles.

Analgesic A pain-relieving drug.

Anaphylaxis An exaggerated, often serious, allergic reaction to proteins and other substances.

Anemia A deficiency in red blood corpuscles or in hemoglobin content of the red corpuscles.

Anesthesia Total or partial loss of sensation from an injection, ingestion or inhalation of a drug.

Anesthesiologist A physician specializing in providing an anesthetic during surgery and monitoring person's vital signs.

Aneurysm A swollen or distended area in a blood vessel wall.

Angiogram X-ray studies in which a dye is injected into the bloodstream to detect abnormalities in blood vessels, tissues and organs.

Antacid A substance that neutralizes acid.

Antibiotic Drugs that check the growth of bacteria but do not work against viruses.

Antibody A substance produced in our bodies to fight against disease organisms.

Assets All of a person's properties, including real estate, cash, stocks and bonds, art, furniture etc., and claims against other people (e.g. loans).

Atrophy A wasting or withering away of part of a body.

Autopsy An examination of a dead body to determine the cause of death; the post-mortem ordered by coroner or medical examiner.

Barbiturate A type of sleeping pill.

Barium Enema Radiopaque barium (visible by x-ray) is put into the lower bowel (colon) and rectum by an enema for an x-ray. Also called a Lower GI Series.

Bed Sore Sore caused by pressure-induced skin ulceration as a result of inadequate blood circulation to the skin. For persons confined to bed, good skin care, repositioning, cushioning and some limited activity are the best treatment.

Beneficiary Person who receives a benefit from a will, insurance policy or trust fund.

Benign A growth that is not cancerous (non-malignant) and does not spread to other parts of the body.

b.i.d. abbrev. = twice a day.

Biopsy The microscopic examination of a portion of body tissue to help in diagnosis. Tissue removed from body by surgery, insertion of needle into tissue and other methods.

Blood Gas Test A blood test to determine the level of oxygen and carbon dioxide in the blood.

Bone Marrow Test A needle is inserted into a bone (hipbone or breastbone) to remove a sample of bone marrow for diagnostic purposes e.g. to diagnose leukemia, aplastic anemia.

Brain Scan More properly called carotid angiogram. A radioactive substance is injected into a neck artery for a brain x-ray using a scanning camera.

CAT Scan A Computerized Axial Tomography scan. A body or head, computer-driven x-ray that gives slice-by-slice view of region.

CCU Coronary Care Unit in a hospital which provides intensive care of heart patients.

Carbohydrates Best source of energy for your body found in most foods but especially sugars and starches. If you eat too much, however, your body changes and stores them as fats.

Cancer A malignant tumor that tends to invade healthy tissue and spread to new sites.

Cardiac Surgeon Physicians specializing in heart surgery.

Cardiologist Physician specializing in diagnosis and treatment of heart conditions.

Cardiovascular Surgeon Physician specializing in surgery of blood vessels associated with the heart.

c.c. abbrev. = cubic centimetre.

Cerebral Palsy Impaired muscular power and coordination from failure of nerve cells in the brain.

Chemotherapy Drug therapy against infection or cancer designed to kill or stop the growth of cancer cells.

Chiropractor Non-physicians specializing in manipulation of the spine; cannot prescribe medication or perform surgery.

Chronic A prolonged or lingering condition.

COPD Chronic Obstructive Pulmonary (Lung) Disease. Includes such illnesses as emphysema.

Colostomy A surgical opening from the body surface (usually through the abdomen) into the colon which acts as an artificial anus. Colostomy bags collect the body's waste. Depending on a person's condition a colostomy may be temporary.

Coma A deep, prolonged unconsciousness.

Congenital Something present since birth.

Cystoscopy A long flexible tube, attached to a miniature camera, is passed through the urinary tract into the bladder to get a direct view for diagnosis and possible treatment. Avoids need for exploratory surgery.

d. abbrev. = give.

dd. in d abbrev. = from day to day.

dec abbrev. = pour off.

Dementia Deterioration of a person's mental capacity from changes in the brain.

Depressant A drug to reduce mental or physical activity.

Dermatologist Physician specializing in skin conditions.

Diagnosis An analysis of someone's physical and/or mental condition.

dil abbrev. = dilute.

Disp. abbrev. = dispense.

Diuretic A drug to increase urine output, relieving edema.

Doctor Common title for a physician. Technically a doctor holds the highest academic degree awarded by a university in fields as different as Doctor of Music, Doctor of Divinity or Doctor of English.

dos abbrev. = dose.

Draw Sheet A normal bed sheet folded in half or thirds and laid across the bed with the long ends dangling over the side of the bed. The sheet can then be used by two people, one at each side of the bed, to lift the person in bed using the draw sheet to raise or lower their body position or to help them turn in bed.

dur dolor abbrev. = while pain lasts.

Dx abbrev. = diagnosis.

ECG See EKG.

EKG (Electrocardiogram) A record of the minute electrical current produced by the heart. Of value in diagnosing abnormal cardiac rhythm and myocardial damage. Also ECG.

EEG (Electroencephalogram) A record of the minute electrical current produced by the brain.

Edema Excess collection of fluid in the tissues.

Electrolyte Substance able to conduct electrical Electrolytes need to be in balance otherwise the person may become quite weak or lose consciousness.

Embolism Blockage of a blood artery by a clot. In the brain it can cause a stroke.

EMG (Electromyography) Test to evaluate the electrical activity of nerves and muscles.

emp abbrev. = as directed.

Emphysema A condition of the lungs marked by labored breathing and increased susceptibility to infection. Includes the loss of elasticity and function of lungs.

Endocrinologist A specialist in diagnosing and treating disorders of the endocrine glands (glands affecting hormones) and their secretions.

Enema A fluid injected into the rectum to clean out the bowel or to administer drugs.

Family Practitioner Physician who diagnoses and treats the general illnesses and problems of people and refers them to a specialist when necessary.

febris Latin for fever.

FRCP[C] abbreviated title for Fellow of the Royal College of Physicians. [C] represents Canadian College. Requires a further four years training after a M.D. degree and denotes a non-surgical specialist.

FRCS[C] abbreviated title for Fellow of the Royal College of Surgeons. [C] represents Canadian College. Requires a further four years training after a M.D. degree and denotes a surgical specialist.

Gastroenterologist Physician specializing in the digestive system: esophagus, stomach, and bowels.

Geneticist Specialist in genetic diseases — hereditary disorders and abnormalities.

Geriatrician Specialist in the diagnoses and treatment of illnesses in older people.

GI (Gastrointestinal) Series An x-ray examination of the esophagus, stomach, colon and rectum.

gm. abbrev. = grams.

gr. abbrev. = grains.

gtt. abbrev. = drops.

h abbrev. = hour.

Hematologist Physician specializing in conditions of the blood.

Hematoma Swelling caused by bleeding into tissues as in a bruise.

Hemiplegia One-sided paralysis of the body, usually from a stroke. A right-sided paralysis indicates left-sided brain damage.

Hemoglobin The protein in red blood cells that carry oxygen to the body tissues.

Hemorrhage Extensive bleeding.

Hereditary Something inherited from parents.

High Blood Pressure *See* Hypertension.

Hodgkin's Disease A form of lymphoid cancer that has high fever, enlarged lymph nodes and spleen, liver and kidneys and a dangerously lowered resistance to infection.

Hormone A glandular excretion into the blood that stimulates another organ.

Hospice Same word as *palliative care.* More recently it refers to community or free- standing institutions where palliative care is given to people with a terminal illness. Programs often have major home care component and may also be part of an established institution such as a hospital.

h.s. abbrev. = at bedtime, before retiring. From the Latin *hora somni.*

Huntington's Chorea A hereditary condition with symptoms of uncontrolled movements and progressive mental disorder.

Hypertension High arterial blood pressure with no apparent symptoms; can lead to a stroke, heart failure or other serious condition if not treated. The pressure measures the force of the blood expelled from the heart against the walls of the blood vessels.

Hypnotic A drug used to induce sleep.

Hypnotism A diagnostic or psychotherapeutic treatment to put a person into a sleep-like trance that enhances memory or makes the person susceptible to suggestion. Can be used in pain relief and to eliminate some negative habits.

Hypotension Low arterial blood pressure.

I&O abbrev. = intake and output refers to fluids into and out of body.

Iatrogenic Disease A condition caused by a doctor.

ICU Intensive Care Unit within a hospital where seriously ill or post-operative patients receive intensified care.

Incontinence Lack of bladder or rectal control so that the person may soil themselves and their bed.

in d abbrev. = daily. From the Latin *in dies*.

Infarction Blockage of a blood vessel especially the artery leading to the heart.

Infection Inflammation or disease caused when bacteria, viruses and other micro-organisms invade the body.

Inflammation Swelling or irritation of tissue.

Insomnia An inability to sleep.

Intern An advanced student or recent medical school graduate undergoing supervised practical training.

Internist Physician who specializes in the nonsurgical treatment of the internal organs of the body.

IV abbrev. = intravenous in which a needle is kept within a vein for the injection of medication.

Laxative A drug to induce bowel movements.

Leukemia Cancer of white blood cells in which these cells reproduce abnormally and inhibit red cell formation.

Lumbar Puncture A diagnostic procedure in which a hollow needle is inserted between two lumbar vertebrae in the spinal cord to remove some spinal fluid.

Lymph Glands Nodes of tissue that provide a system of protection against bacteria and other attacks against the body's immune system.

m et n abbrev. = morning and night.

Malignant Cancer growth of a tumor and may also spread (*metastasize)* to other parts of the body. May be life-threatening.

Malnutrition Insufficient consumption of essential food elements whether by improper diet or illness.

Mammography An x-ray of the breasts to detect presence of tumors and whether tumor is malignant or benign.

Meningitis Inflammation of the membranes covering and protecting the brain and spinal cord.

Metastasis The spreading of an infection or cancer from its original area to others throughout the body.

mg. abbrev. = milligrams.

mor dict abbrev. = in the manner directed.

Multiple Sclerosis A degenerative disease of the central nervous system in which the tissues harden.

Muscular Dystrophy A degenerative muscular disease in which muscles waste away.

Neoplasm A tumor or a new growth of abnormal tissue that has uncontrolled cell multiplication. *See* Cancer.

Nephrologist Physician specializing in kidney conditions.

Neurologist Physician specializing in the nervous system.

Neurosurgeon Physician specializing in surgery of the nervous system.

non rep abbrev. = do not repeat.

notarize A notary public authenticates or attests to the truth of a document (i.e. attests that a document was signed by a particular person).

notary public A public officer (can be a lawyer) who certifies documents, takes affidavits and administers oaths.

Nurse Practitioner Registered Nurse who has received additional training in order to perform more specialized medical care than other nurses.

o abbrev. = none.

Obstetrician/Gynecologist Physician specializing in conditions of the female reproductive system. Obstetrician specializes in pregnancies and births.

Oncologist Physician specializing in tumors and cancer.

Ophthalmologist Physician who specializes in diseases of the eye.

Optician Non-physician trained in filling prescriptions for eyeglasses and contact lens.

Optometrist Non-physician trained to measure vision and make eyeglasses and contact lens.

Orthopedist Physician specializing in bones.

Osteopathy The diagnoses and treatment of disorders by manipulative therapy, drugs, surgery, proper diet and psychotherapy to prevent disease and restore health. Not approved in all jurisdictions but where permitted, must be licensed.

Osteoporosis A weakening of the bones through a loss of calcium and occurs most often in old age.

Otolaryngologist A specialist in conditions of the ear, throat and nose.

Palliative Care Treatment to relieve symptoms, rather than cure, a disease or condition. In modern sense includes the physical, emotional, spiritual and informational supports of people who are dying. Also called hospice care.

Paracentesis Fluid drainage by insertion of a tube into the body.

Parkinson's Disease A progressive nervous disease of the latter years. Symptoms are muscular tremor, slowing of movement, partial facial paralysis and impaired motor control.

Pathologist Physician who examines tissue and bone to diagnose if malignancy exists. They also perform autopsies.

Pathology The scientific study of disease.

pc abbrev. = after meals.

Pediatrician Physician specializing in the care of children.

pH Test Determines the degree of acidity or alkalinity in urine.

Physiatrist Physician specializing in rehabilitative therapy after illness or injury. Uses exercise, massage, water and heat to restoring useful activities to a person.

Physician A medical doctor as opposed to people with a Ph.D. who are also called Doctor.

Placebo A substance containing no medication. It can help a person who believes that it will work. A practical and effective treatment for some people.

Plasma The liquid part of blood (55% of total volume).

Plastic Surgeon Physician specializing in reconstructive surgery such as victims of major accidents.

Pneumonia An acute or chronic disease which inflames the lungs with associated fluid collection.

p.o. abbrev. = by mouth. From the Latin *per os*.

Podiatrist Non-physician who specializes in the care, treatment and surgery of feet.

prn abbrev. = as needed, as often as necessary.

Proctologist Physician specializing in diagnoses and treatment of disorders and diseases of anus, colon and rectum.

Prognosis (Prog. or Px) Prediction of the future course of a condition or illness based upon scientific study. It is only a prediction and should not be accepted as fact.

Prosthesis An artificial substitute for a part of our body such as an arm or leg.

Psychiatrist Physician who specializes in the diagnosis and treatment of emotional and medical disorders; may prescribe medication.

Psychologist A professional with a Ph.D. in psychology who diagnoses and treats psychological disorders. They may not prescribe medication.

pt abbrev. = patient.

Px abbrev. = prognosis.

q abbrev. = every.

q.h. abbrev. = every hour. From the Latin *quaque hora*.

q.i.d. abbrev. = four times a day. From the Latin *quater in die*.

qn abbrev. = every night. From the Latin *quaque nox*.

qod abbrev. = every other day.

qs abbrev. = proper amount, quantity sufficient.

Quack Opportunist who uses highly questionable or worthless methods or devices in diagnosing and treating various diseases.

ql abbrev. = as much as desired. From the Latin *quantum libet*.

Radiologist Physician who interprets X-rays. Sub-specialties include nuclear medicine and angiography.

Radiology A branch of science using radiant energy, as in x-rays, especially in the diagnosis and treatment of disease.

Regimen A program or set of rules to follow for treatment of a condition.

rep abbrev. = repeat.

Resident Physician receiving specialized clinical training.

Respirologist Specialist who diagnoses and treats diseases of lungs and respiratory (breathing) system.

Rheumatologist Specialist who diagnoses and treats rheumatic diseases characterized by inflammation or pain in the joints and muscles.

Rx abbrev. = prescription or therapy.

Senility Loss of mental ability and memory (especially of recent events). Age related deterioration of brain cells.

Shiatsu *See* Acupressure.

Shock Sudden, acute failure of body's circulatory function.

sig abbrev. = write, let it be imprinted.

Spinal Tap *See* Lumbar Puncture.

stat abbrev. = right away, immediately. From the Latin *statim.*

Stroke (Apoplexy) Sudden loss of muscular control, sensation and consciousness resulting from rupture or blocking of a blood vessel in the brain.

Suppository A medication given in solid form and inserted into the rectum or vagina. Dissolves into a liquid by body heat.

Surgeon Physician who treats a disease by surgical operations. Surgeons generally specialize in one or more types of surgery.

Symptom An indication of a certain condition or disease.

Syndrome A group of symptoms that indicate a specific disease or condition.

Temperature Normal oral temperature is 97-99 degrees Fahrenheit or 36-37.2 degrees Celsius. Changes +/- one degree during day.

Thoracic Surgeon Physician who specializes in chest surgery.

t.i.d. abbrev. = three times a day. From the Latin *tres in die.*

Toxin A poison or harmful agent.

Tumor *See* Neoplasm.

Tx abbrev. = treatment.

Ultrasound Scan A picture of internal organs by using high frequency sound waves.

Urologist Physicians specializing in urinary tract and male prostrate gland diseases plus male sexual dysfunction. Although they treat non-surgical patients they also operate on kidneys and do prostate resectioning/removal.

ut dict abbrev. = as directed.

Vascular Surgeon Physician specializing in blood vessel surgery.

Vital Signs Measurement of temperature, pulse and respiration rate.

Vomiting A reflex action that contracts the stomach and ejects contents through the mouth.

X-ray Electromagnetic radiation used to create photographic pictures of the body's internal structures.

X-ray Dye A substance injected into a vein prior to an X-ray to highlight an area for examination. May cause an allergic reaction.

White blood cells Cells which fight infection. The normal count is 5,000 to 10,000.

Add your own definitions, descriptions and abbreviations here for future reference.

General Reference List

Call 1-800-387-1417 (or fax 416-924-3383) to order any of the following books from The Albert Britnell Book Shop. Expect 4-8 week delivery delay unless you ask it to be couriered to you. *Also check with your local library, book store, home care coordinator, visiting home nurse and family physician for any resources they may have.*

For information on specific illnesses or conditions, check the reference sections in some of the books listed below or ask for up-to-date information from the specific association that represents that illness or condition. For example, the Cancer Society, Heart and Stroke Associations, ALS Society, AIDS Committees, etc. are all listed in your local or provincial capital telephone books.

Appearance Concepts Foundation of Canada. (1990). **Changes, Choices and Challenges**. Toronto: Appearance Concepts Foundation of Canada. *This book gives practical information on using scarfs and wigs to cover one's head as well as information on skin care for women who have undergone radiation or chemotherapy.*

Callwood, June. (1986). **Twelve Weeks in Spring**. Toronto: Lester and Orpen Dennys. *The story of how 60 friends and colleagues took care of Margaret Frazer in her own home.*

Chilnick, Lawrence D. (Editor-in-Chief). (most recent edition). **The Pill Book**. New York: Bantam Books. *Alphabetical listing and illustrated guide to most medications in U.S.*

Conolly, Matthew and Orme, Michael. (1988). **The Patients' Desk Reference**. New York: Prentice Hall Press. *Lists thousands of medications indexed by illness or condition.*

Duda, Deborah. (1987). **Coming Home: A Guide to Dying at Home with Dignity**. New York: Aurora Press. *A 400-page reference text for families.*

First Aid Books: Any first aid book (and course!) to help keep you up-to-date on emergency procedures, CPR and mouth-to-mouth resuscitation.

Foundation for Canadians Facing Cancer. *Facing Cancer with Confidence* (18-minute video tape). 2075 Bayview Avenue, Toronto, Ontario, M4N 3M5; 1-800-387-9954.

Haller, James. (1994). **What to Eat When You Don't Feel Like Eating.** Hantsport, Nova Scotia: Robert Pope Foundation. *A cookbook designed for people preparing food for others who are suffering a serious illness.*

Larson, David E. (Editor-in-Chief). (1990) **Mayo Clinic Family Health Book**. New York: William Morrow and Company. *Extensive, illustrated home medical reference from prevention, tests, treatment alternatives and more.*

Mace, Nancy L and Rabins, Peter V. (1981). **The 36-Hour Day: A Family Guide to Caring for Persons with Alzheimer's Disease, Related Dementing Illnesses, and Memory Loss in Later Life**. New York: Warner Books. *373-page text for families.*

Perry, Anne and Potter, Patricia A. (1986). **Pocket Nurse Guide to Basic Skills and Procedures**. Toronto: C.V. Mosby. *More complete information on all the techniques suggested in this book and much more — from a nurse's perspective.*

Portnow, Jay with Houtmann, Martha. (1987). **Home Care for the Elderly**. New York: Pocket Books (Simon and Schuster). *263-page text for families.*

St. John Ambulance. (most recent edition). **The Complete Handbook of Family Health Care**. Ottawa: The Priory of Canada of The Most Venerable Order of The Hospital of St. John of Jerusalem. *Short, yet thorough, review of family health care.*

Tkac, Debora (General Editor). (1990). **The Doctors Book of Home Remedies**. Emmaus, PA: Rodale Press. *Thousands of tips and techniques anyone can use to heal everyday health problems.*

Thompson, Wendy. (1987). **Aging is a Family Affair: A Guide to Quality Visiting, Long Term Care Facilities and You**. Toronto: NC Press. *164-page guide for families.*

van Bommel, Harry. (1993). **Choices for People Who Have a Terminal Illness, Their Families and Their Caregivers**. Toronto: NC Press Limited. *192 pages with charts and forms to help take care of people at home..*

Whiting Little, Deborah. (1985). **Home Care for the Dying**. New York: Doubleday. *315-page reference text for families.*

Finding Out about Local Home Care Programs

Home care is a group of services which enables people to live at home, often with the result that people do not have to remain in, or return as often to, a hospital or a long-term care facility. Basic home care services may include:

- ❑ visiting nursing
- ❑ home support (help with homemaking such as light housekeeping, shopping, cooking)
- ❑ physical therapy
- ❑ occupational therapy
- ❑ respiratory therapy
- ❑ social work counselling
- ❑ nutrition counselling
- ❑ housing registry
- ❑ personal emergency response systems.

More complex services may include:

- ❑ home intravenous antibiotic therapy
- ❑ life support/ventilator assistance systems
- ❑ services for children with complex needs
- ❑ tube feedings (either by nose or through the stomach wall)
- ❑ home cancer therapy
- ❑ palliative/hospice care
- ❑ care for people who have some form of dementia.

Community support services may include:

- ❑ adult day centres
- ❑ meals-on-wheels and/or wheels to meals programs
- ❑ respite care (care for family caregivers to give them some time off)

- ❑ transportation help
- ❑ help with shopping
- ❑ help with home maintenance.

Home care programs across Canada and the United States provide different services. To find out what is available in your community, you can check with your family physician, community health office, or other home health care providers. If a particular service is not available in your community, ask your political leadership why and how your community can arrange to get such service in the near future. If you have difficulty in finding out what services are available, you can contact:

Canadian Home Care Association
Suite 401
17 York Street
Ottawa, Ontario
K1N 9J6
CANADA
Phone (613) 569-1585

National Association for Home Care
228 7th Street South East
Washington, DC
20003
USA
Phone (202) 547-7424

INDEX

Important Information

"What I want done in case of emergency."

The following is a list of people I can call or visit for help. (Your family physician, home care case manager or visiting home nurse will help you fill out the information that you do not know.)

Your Own Immediate Family not living with you

Family Physician

Specialists

Home Care Contact Person

Visiting Home Nurses

Homemaking Program

Volunteer Support Programs

Person's Health Card Number and related Insurance Numbers

NOTES